WILD FOR LOVE

Polly is an ecologist, passionate and uncompromising about wildlife rights. Against all her principles she falls in love with Jake, heir to a London media empire, whose development company is about to destroy a beautiful marsh. But can love ever blossom between two such different people? As Polly battles to save the marsh and learns to compromise for love, Jake finally finds the life he has always desired . . .

ALL HOPE LOST

CAROL MacLEAN

WILD FOR LOVE

Complete and Unabridged

LINFORD
Leicester

First published in Great Britain in 2009

First Linford Edition
published 2011

British Library CIP Data

MacLean, Carol.
  Wild for love. - -
  (Linford romance library)
  1. Women ecologists- -Fiction.
  2. Real estate development- -
  Environmental aspects- -Fiction.
  3. Love stories. 4. Large type books.
  I. Title II. Series
  823.9'2–dc22

  ISBN 978-1-4448-0922-0

Published by
F. A. Thorpe (Publishing)
Anstey, Leicestershire

Set by Words & Graphics Ltd.
Anstey, Leicestershire
Printed and bound in Great Britain by
T. J. International Ltd., Padstow, Cornwall

This book is printed on acid-free paper

1

Polly shrieked as a sudden rush of icy cold water poured over the tops of her Wellington boots and filled them. The bottle trap slipped from her wet fingers and bobbed merrily away across the loch. As if on cue, it started to rain heavily.

'This was not the forecast,' she yelled to the darkening sky. Her usually curly red hair was plastered flat to her skin and she shoved an angry hand across her face to get it out of her eyes. What had started as a simple wildlife survey for great crested newts was turning into a major catastrophe.

She was standing in the shallows of the pond where she had been searching for newts' eggs on the broad leaves of water mint. The plan had been to carry out the survey, set some traps for adult newts and have a walk around the site. But as she bent to set the traps, she noticed a moorhen with a broken wing paddling not far from her. If she could catch it, she could take it to the rescue centre where they could fix the bird's bones. She moved cautiously into slightly deeper water, then launched herself towards the poor bird. It gave an indignant squawk and flew off, trailing one wing but still successfully airborne.

Polly sighed. She looked around her at the beautiful countryside and her heart sank at the thought of what was planned for it. In every direction, stretching for miles, grassland and small copses of woodland surrounded a huge loch and a marsh with smaller ponds scattered in the midst of it. The scenery was idyllic and burgeoning with all kinds of wildlife. The most amazing thing about it was that the city of Glasgow was only a few miles away, hidden from Polly's view by a gentle rise of small hillocks topped with old oaks. To someone who enjoyed the outdoors, it was a wonderful place to hike and watch for birds. There were plenty of trails made by both people and roe deer criss-crossing the rough grassland, idling by the pools and wandering through the trees. A few old farm buildings were dotted about but most were disused and crumbling into disrepair.

With the city encroaching steadily, farming was no longer an option. Now there were plans to build a huge housing estate on the greenbelt land. The loch would be filled in, the marsh would be drained and the woods chopped down. A man-made jungle of brick and Tarmac would replace it all.

Polly had been hired as an ecologist by Rathbone Development Company to look for rare and protected animals which would have to be considered in their planning applications. Although it would appear she was working for the enemy, Polly knew it was the only way that the wildlife could be saved before building work went ahead. She was determined to find everything there was to find.

Except that it looked as if the day was ruined. The rain was coming down in sheets, and Polly could feel it hitting her scalp. It trickled horribly down the back of her neck, and her body and legs were also soaked in spite of her waterproof coat and leggings. Her feet were swimming in their boots, and felt incredibly heavy because her woolly socks had taken up so much loch water. With alarm, she realised that the shallow edge of the loch was no longer calf-deep. The water was running swiftly now over her knees with surprising power. Glancing up, she saw that the stream joining the loch had swollen rapidly with the rainwater and was gushing and bubbling furiously in its efforts to find the loch. The water level was rising fast.

In a panic, Polly saw that the bottle trap was now a tiny white dot in the distance as the current moved it further and further away from the edge. She tried to move her heavy legs and feet back towards dry land but they would not budge. Her boots were stuck firmly in the mud.

'Come on!' she said urgently to herself. 'Get out of here.'

With all her strength she pulled again with her feet, bending down and using her hands to grip the rim of one boot under the icy water. No deal. The soles were firmly entrenched in the black ooze. Polly could smell the stink of the bacterial mud, blending with the crushed herb scent of water mint and above all the smell of cold pond water.

She looked around her at the now gloomy landscape, darkly streaked with rain. There was no point in crying for help because there was absolutely no-one around.

'That's because no-one is as stupid as you,' she told herself tightly, feeling her heart beat fast and jumpily as she realised that her situation was becoming dangerous.

At that moment there was a clap of

thunder, swiftly followed by a shard of lightning splintering off the nearby hills.

If the storm moved any closer, she realised with a jolt, then the lightning could hit the loch. She looked down at her legs. Would her rubber boots be enough to save her? Polly did not know. She only knew that she didn't want to find out.

Carefully, trying not to overbalance, she pulled her right leg out of the boot and set it down slowly in the loch hoping that it too would not stick. She pulled her left leg clear and was just about to stand up when the mud gave way and she slipped forward. With a scream, Polly toppled headfirst into the loch. The shock of cold water was like a slap to the face. She took in a mouthful and spat it out. Coughing and ploughing with her arms to stay afloat, Polly saw the grass where she had stood only that morning receding. The current was taking her out after the bottle float!

'Help! Help!' she shouted. The current turned her round and her heavy clothes were dragging her down. There was a very real chance that she would drown. Polly thought of her parents and sister; how angry they would be that she had wasted her life in such a silly incident. The thought of Lou's sorrow gave her extra strength, and Polly started shouting as loudly as she could until her throat was raw. After a while, when there was no answering call, she got tired. Her limbs ached and were numb from the cold. She was slowing down.

'I must have a little rest,' she thought fuzzily and let herself relax.

She sank gently, head hanging down. It was very peaceful underwater. Sounds were muted. Her arms and legs felt as if they belonged to someone else. She needed a breath. She opened her lips to take a fatal mouthful of water. But suddenly she was grabbed painfully by the collar of her jacket. Bright lights flashed in front of her eyes, and she was rudely manhandled from the peace of the water and

7

thrown onto the hard ground. Before she had a chance to recover, warm lips were on hers, breathing into her, and her chest was pummelled. Polly woke up to the world again, rolled over, coughed once and was promptly sick onto someone's shoes.

'That's much better,' said a deep voice beside her. Polly groaned. Her head hurt. She felt terrible. She sat up gingerly and felt a strong arm supporting her. Attempting to focus on her rescuer, Polly was aware of two intensely blue eyes staring at her with concern from under dark brows.

'We'd better get you to a hospital,' the man said, lifting her to her feet and continuing to support her with his arms.

Polly was suddenly aware of his body heat and his height as he loomed over her. She looked up at him and saw a firm jaw, stubbled as if he had not shaved that day. His hair was chestnut, catching the light as the day finally relinquished the storm and brightened into a reasonable late spring warmth.

She noticed the way his hair curled over his collar just a little. *If left to its own devices*, Polly thought hazily, *he would have hair just as curly as her own.*

'You need to stay awake,' the man ordered. Polly stumbled and was caught in his strong grip. He sighed deeply. Then, before she could protest, he had swung her up in his arms and was striding across country towards a battered vehicle parked on the far road.

She began to feel better as they drove back towards the city.

'I don't need a hospital,' she said.

He looked at her sceptically before returning his sharp gaze to the road and the increasing traffic.

'Really,' Polly repeated. 'If you could please just drop me at my flat.'

She gave him directions and sat shivering. Her head certainly felt clearer but her muscles seemed to be in spasm and the shivering would not stop.

She spent the short journey with her teeth chattering. Boy, was she cold. They drew up in front of her tenement door. Polly fumbled with the door lock but her fingers would not work.

The man opened the door and helped her out.

'I'll take you up. You need dry clothes and heat, fast.'

Polly didn't argue. She was severely chilled. She would never manage to get the house keys into the lock, in any case. Her flatmate, Keisha, was out of town for the weekend so the flat was empty. She left him in her tiny kitchen, putting the kettle on. He seemed to fill the room with his broad shoulders. One steaming hot shower later, Polly began to feel like a human being again. Dressed in fresh jeans and a sweatshirt, she came back downstairs to find he had made a pot of tea and discovered some biscuits.

'How do you feel?' he asked.

She heard the rebuke in his tone and looked up at him, puzzled.

'Much better, thanks. Look, I won't hold you up any longer. I've taken enough time out of your day.'

'You little idiot!' he said sharply. 'You act as if that incident was nothing but an inconvenience. You could have been killed.'

'Well, I wasn't,' Polly snapped back.

She was shaking again now but this time it was with anger, not with cold. How dare he get annoyed with her? What business was it of his, anyway?

'I didn't ask you to get involved,' she added childishly.

He snorted dismissively. 'I suppose you were just on the verge of pulling yourself out,' he said, his voice heavy with sarcasm. 'I'm sorry I interfered.'

She glared up at him. 'It was a freak accident. I'm not some foolish girl wandering around marshes looking for trouble. I have years of experience of wilderness hiking, and I had all the right gear.'

'You may have had all the correct equipment but what on earth were you doing, up to your thighs in swamp water?'

His tone was one of disbelief. He

obviously thought that she *was* a foolish girl, in spite of her fine words.

'It was up to my knees,' she informed him coolly.

If my hair would stop bouncing about in a riot of curls, Polly thought, *it would give me an awful lot more dignity. Then this irritating man would have to take me seriously.* She tucked a stray piece behind her ear and saw his blue eyes watching. He stood waiting for an answer. Well, he would have to do without the truth, Polly decided, as a description of surveying for great crested newts was likely to take much longer than making something up.

'I saw something interesting in the water,' she improvised, hoping he wouldn't ask what.

He raised an eyebrow, and the twitch of his lips suggested the merest hint of amusement. *Well, he can laugh at me all he wants*, thought Polly, *as long as he stops staring at me in that disconcerting way.*

'May I suggest that, next time you

see something interesting in the water,' he said softly, 'you look to make sure there isn't a flash flood coming close behind.'

Polly flushed. He seemed to loom over her, with his broad shoulders and tall frame. What was he, six foot two at least? And those eyes — so piercing. As if they could see all her secrets, all her faults.

He leaned towards her, and for an instant Polly was sure he was going to kiss her. She could feel the heat of him, see his firm jaw and imagine running her hands through his thick, copper hair. She turned her face up to him, already anticipating his lips upon hers and ready to abandon herself to his embrace. He frowned down at her and touched her lightly on the nose.

'You've got a few cuts there. Make sure you put antiseptic on them.'

Deflated, Polly took a step back and almost fell into the armchair. What was wrong with her today? Why was this man having such an effect on her? He was being perfectly polite and had saved her from a terrible situation and all she could think about was being kissed passionately by him. Perhaps it was simply a fever brought on by her immersion.

'Tea, Mr — ?' she said weakly.

'It's Jake,' he replied, looking at her with some concern. 'You don't look too good. I think I should go now and you should tuck yourself up in bed.'

So much for romance. She was getting all hot and bothered about him, while he was treating her like a small child!

She pulled herself together. 'I'm Polly.'

'Well, Polly, nice to meet you. Try not to have any more adventures today.' He grinned suddenly, which made him look younger and somewhat rakish. 'I'll let myself out.'

It was only once he had gone and Polly had snuggled down under the duvet that she realised she did not know his surname and had no way of finding him again.

2

Polly groaned as she looked in the bathroom mirror the next morning. Not only was she going to be late for work, but she looked terrible. Whatever branches and submerged litter she had bumped against as she sank to the bottom of the loch had scraped her face and left scratches across her nose and cheeks. A night's sleep had only made them redder. She stuck a plaster over the worst cut on the bridge of her nose, made a face at herself in the mirror, which made her wince, and brushed her unruly hair as best she could. When it was secured with combs and her make-up was applied, Polly began to feel better. She ate a quick breakfast and ran to catch the bus.

Green Lives Consultancy was based on the fifth floor of a newly-built Clydeside office block in the heart of

Glasgow. The building was mostly gleaming glass, with a tiny circle of bright green grass roof on top of a sandstone tower incorporated into the attractive design. Polly loved the place. It was right on the edge of a busy street and opposite the River Clyde which teemed with seagulls and pedestrians all day. There was always something to see. The interminable noise of the traffic stopped as soon as she flung herself through the revolving door and with a quick wave to Tony, the concierge, she ran two steps at a time up to floor five.

Neil Gardner was already at his desk, tapping away at his keyboard, when Polly arrived. She threw her bag down on her chair and poured herself a large, strong coffee from the filter machine that stood conveniently outside her tiny office room.

'Did the other guy win?' asked Neil with a grin.

'Does it look so bad?'

'Pretty awful. What on earth happened?'

'You won't want to hear this, Neil, but I ended up going to Monmeir Loch by myself and fell in.'

Neil's grin faded instantly, to be replaced by a scowl. 'You know the rules, Polly — there must always be two people out surveying. It's basic health and safety. What got into you?'

'Harriet was sick, and I wanted to get the work done before the meeting with the developers today. I had hoped to have some results to show them to back up my argument for saving the loch.'

Neil shook his head in exasperation. 'You don't always have to give two hundred percent in your work, Polly. One hundred would do nicely. I would rather have you alive and not bruised and battered. I can wait another few days for your report.'

'You know as well as I do, Neil, that Raymond Rathbone will be working overtime to get his planning permissions for that development. Even if that means draining the entire marsh and killing all the wildlife. We have simply got to get evidence of special species to save Monmeir!'

Neil sighed. Sometimes Polly's zeal and principles made his own ecological beliefs seem rather weak.

'We *will* get the evidence. But let's take our time and not kill ourselves over it. And remember that at the end of the day, it's Raymond Rathbone who is paying our wages this month. We may be a consultancy but we do have to bend to the wishes of whoever is hiring us.'

'So we give him his money's worth,' retorted Polly.

'Anyway, you can forget about Rathbone for the moment. Apparently he has fallen ill rather suddenly. It's his nephew who will be coming up from London for today's progress meeting.'

They both turned at the sound of the door opening. Harriet had arrived, complete with a red nose and watery eyes.

'Morning,' she croaked, waving a hanky and a bulky paper file at them.

'Sorry I couldn't make it to Monmeir yesterday, Polly, but here's the background information you wanted.'

Harriet was the team's administration support. In a normal office, that would have meant some typing and filing and making cups of tea, but at Green Lives, it meant she was often asked to don Wellington boots and waterproofs and tramp about the countryside in all weathers making notes and annotating maps. She loved it.

'Did I hear you mention Jacob Grayling?' Her eyes brightened and she blew her nose enthusiastically.

'Rathbone's nephew,' said Neil, for Polly's benefit. He ran his fingers through his spiky hair and retreated behind his computer screen. Harriet loved to gossip. Let Polly bear the brunt.

'You *must* have heard of him,' Harriet said, nodding at Polly.

'I depend on you for all my latest celeb news.' Polly grimaced.

'His photo's been in all the celebrity magazines this week. He's heir to the Grayling media empire. Shanna Grayling is his mother.'

'Well, no wonder he gets his photos in the magazines if his mummy owns them, is there!'

'That's not why. He makes a good story in his own right. Always has a different gorgeous woman by his side. He jet-sets all over the world. He's a partner in his uncle's business, but that's rather dull so the magazines don't really go into detail on that. But he *does* know a lot of famous people.' Harriet sighed happily.

'He sounds rather dull himself,' remarked Polly, 'if all he does is get publicity through being seen with other people. What a shallow person.'

The phone rang just as she finished her initial report on Monmeir Loch.

'Polly, it's Lou here. Can you come round? I really need you.'

Polly opened her mouth to remind her sister that she was at work, and then shut it again slowly. There was a note of desperation in Lou's voice.

She could get to Lou's house and make it back to the meeting if she was quick, she decided. Before going, she peeled the plaster off her nose and added another layer of make-up. Lou would only fuss if she heard about what Polly had been up to.

★   ★   ★

Lou and her husband Ian lived in a quiet suburb on the south side of Glasgow. The houses were all well-kept with immaculate gardens. The only difference between Lou's garden and the others in the street was the rowan tree with its plethora of bird-feeders and a hopeful nestbox. These were gifts from Polly to her three-year-old niece Laura, who loved 'the birdies'. Polly noticed the car was in the driveway, which meant that Ian was home from work. What was going on? With a feeling of dread, Polly rang the doorbell.

Lou answered the door immediately. The sisters were like chalk and cheese in looks; where Polly was small and curvaceous, Lou was tall and thin. In contrast to Polly's abundant red curls, Lou had straight, corn-blonde hair. What they had in common, though, was their love for each other. Lou had always been the big sister Polly could rely on and confide in. It distressed her now to see that same big sister looking so pale and drawn.

Polly gave her a fierce hug. 'Whatever it is, Lou, I'll sort it out.'

Lou took her through to the living room. Polly was shocked. It was usually clean and tidy but now the cushions were tumbled on the floor, one of them smeared with jam. Everywhere she looked there were toys, crayons, crumpled paper and dolls. Crumbs and dust collected under the radiator.

'I can't cope any more,' Lou blurted out, watching Polly's gaze. 'I'm so tired, Polly.' She started crying.

For a moment, Polly froze. She hadn't seen Lou cry since they were children and Lou had broken her arm falling out of the big sycamore tree. Their roles had been reversed. Polly had often had the opportunity to cry to Lou about all her problems, and Lou had always helped her. Now it was time to pay that back.

She led Lou over to the sofa, brushed off crumbs, and put the cushions back in place. 'Where's Ian?' she asked gently.

'He's taken Laura out for a walk. She had the most terrible tantrums this morning because I wouldn't give her a biscuit. And Ian blames *me!*'

'Why would he do that?'

Polly couldn't imagine Ian being so cruel. He and Lou were the perfect couple. They'd been married for ten years and had spent that time enjoying each other's company. Why would he turn on Lou for something so trivial?

'He says I give in to her too much, and that I spoil her. He says that he and

I never get a chance to spend time together any more and he's had enough.' Lou was sobbing.

Polly thought for a while. She made tea, and persuaded Lou to calm down enough to drink a cup. She tidied up the living room and put the toys back into Laura's bedroom.

'I've got a solution,' she said at last.

Lou smiled tearfully. 'You always were the practical one, Polly.'

'Maybe Ian's right. You do need time together. I'll take Laura all day Saturday, and you and he can go shopping or to the cinema or whatever.'

'Isn't that the day of the protest march?'

Polly had completely forgotten. She had promised her parents she'd go along and support the campaign to save Croombs Wood. There was no way she could possibly miss it.

'Well, Sunday then.'

Lou nodded grateful acceptance. 'Will you manage her by yourself?'

'No problem. We'll have fun,' said

Polly confidently. How difficult could it be, looking after a three-year-old child?

'Have you ever thought of having kids yourself?' asked Lou curiously. She had often mopped up Polly's tears over relationships, but children had never been mentioned.

'Goodness, no!' Polly laughed. 'I love being an auntie, but I don't think I'm cut out for motherhood. Besides, where would I find a good husband?'

'Is there no-one special in your life?'

Polly had a fleeting image of piercing blue eyes and chestnut hair. She shut it out. She was never likely to see him again. Besides, it made her uneasy to remember just what an impression he had made on her senses.

Lou was looking at her intently.

'All the best men are taken, like Ian,' Polly said lightly.

'I'm not sure any more that he *is* one of the best men.'

'Don't say that, Lou! You and Ian are my ideal when I think of marriage. Like Mum and Dad. You have a lifelong bond. At least one of us has been lucky enough to find that.'

'Don't you ever want to get married?'

'I don't think any man would ever match up to my ideal,' confessed Polly. 'And unless he did, I wouldn't even consider it. I want everlasting love, I want passion *and* I want a soulmate.'

Lou laughed out loud. 'You don't ask for much, do you, fussy little sis?'

'Well, at least I've cheered you up,' answered Polly, grinning. 'I've got to go now, but I will be round on Sunday to collect my darling niece.'

She gave Lou a kiss on the cheek and hurried out.

★ ★ ★

The meeting was being held in a large conference room on the sixth floor. Neil Gardner was already seated at the huge, polished wooden table, his hair even spikier than usual, as if he had run his hands through it many times. He was peering at a map of Monmeir, which was covered in red arrows and scribbled annotations. Harriet was sitting beside him, pen poised to take minutes of the meeting. She smiled valiantly at Polly, then sneezed and was hidden behind her handkerchief.

Polly recognised the architect and building consultant from Rathbone's and they nodded in acknowledgement of her. At the far end of the room, staring out of the plate-glass window at the view across the river with his back to the others, stood a tall man, impeccably dressed in an expensive grey suit. Polly slid into a seat and found her pen and file.

Neil coughed politely. 'Gentlemen, ladies, perhaps we could make a start. I think introductions are in order as Mr Rathbone is unfortunately unwell and Mr Grayling is standing in for him.'

Polly wrote the date and meeting title neatly at the top of her fresh, blank page. She vaguely heard Neil introducing her as Miss Pauline Baker. Then her heart missed a beat as a deep and familiar voice said, 'Miss Baker. Delighted to meet you.'

She looked up into the familiar blue eyes, took in his copper-coloured hair and firm jaw. Time stood still until she became aware she was gaping. Neil and Harriet were looking at her in puzzlement. Polly saw a brief flare of surprise in Jacob Grayling's eyes as he recognised her, then his lips twitched in amusement.

'Let's keep the meeting informal,' he suggested. 'Call me Jake.'

Neil nudged her surreptitiously with his elbow as he began to talk over the map and explain progress to Jake Grayling. Polly's throat felt dry and her heart was now beating faster. Either she had Harriet's cold, or she was coming down with something much worse — a very bad case of attraction.

I am not going to give in to this, Polly told herself silently. *I swore off men after the last fiasco. I am concentrating on my career, remember!* Besides, another look at Jake with his

28

Savile Row suit, crisp white shirt and silk tie, confirmed her gut feelings. He was not for her. Her type had always been rumpled men with beards and long hair, who went on campaigns and very rarely had long-term jobs. They were free spirits, not corporate clones.

'Miss Baker, would you like to tell us your results so far?' Jake asked.

'My initial conclusion is that Monmeir Loch is a very valuable place for wildlife,' answered Polly with emphasis. 'It would be an act of vandalism to drain it and the surrounding marsh and build houses on it.'

There was silence. Neil shuffled papers tensely. He glared at Polly meaningfully. Her role was simply to report on the species and habitats at the moment. The time for interpretation of the facts should be kept for later — and at the discretion of Rathbone Developments.

Polly ignored him. Even though Rathbone was paying their wages, there was no way she could disregard her instincts; she had to tell the truth.

'We are a development company, Miss Baker,' Jake said dryly. 'We build houses, that's how we make our money. You will also remember that the area of Monmeir is, and has been for quite some time, zoned for business development.'

'Well, whoever zoned it, got it wrong,' retorted Polly. How dare he treat her like an idiot? She knew all that. It didn't have to be spelled out.

'People need houses. There is a significant shortage of affordable housing in this area.'

She noticed the other men nodding in agreement. He had an air of authority about him without even trying, she realised with irritation. The other men in the room were head and shoulders shorter than him, but even had they been taller, Polly knew they would have bowed to his commands.

'Save the loch and cut the number of houses in half,' suggested Polly.

There was a ripple of disbelieving

laughter from the architect and building consultant. Jake silenced them with a look.

'That would halve the profits,' he pointed out calmly.

He was torn between annoyance and amusement at the woman. Here she was, working for him, and yet prepared to stand up and defy him with her preposterous ideas. A typical redhead. Not his type at all. He looked at her bright curls which had escaped her tortoiseshell clip and were now framing her delicate face. He noticed that her flashing green eyes with their dark lashes were slightly tilted, like a cat's. He saw the cut across the bridge of her nose, in amongst a scatter of childish freckles, and it reminded him of his first view of her struggling for breath amongst the weeds and brown marsh water. Yes, she was too short and too curvy for his taste. And her colouring was too obvious. It matched her temper.

'Would you ever consider doing the

right thing? Or is everything with you about money?' Polly snapped.

'Doing the right thing?' Jake said coldly. 'That reminds me, Mr Gardner, that we need to have a chat about your health and safety standards. It is certainly not the right thing to send a single woman out to wander about in deep water looking for goodness knows what.'

Neil shuffled his papers nervously and was about to answer when Polly cut in angrily. 'It's not Neil's fault that I was out there. Of course we usually pair up for surveys — we have a very high standard of risk assessment at Green Lives. These were exceptional circumstances.'

She sat fuming for the rest of the meeting while the men discussed planning applications, pored over maps and looked at building designs. She was very aware of Jake's presence at the far end of the table. As the meeting adjourned and everyone filed out, he stopped her.

'I will need you to accompany me to London next week to report to Mr Rathbone directly at the design meeting. Please be ready.'

His manner was impersonal and coldly polite. It was as if he had never sat in her kitchen, pouring tea. She remembered the strength and feel of his arms as he carried her from the loch, then knocked that memory to the back of her mind. If he wanted to act cool and emotionless, then she would too.

'Very well, Mr Grayling,' she answered, deliberately not using his first name. 'I will clear my diary for next week and await your call.'

He started to speak and then thought better of it. He swept up his overcoat and briefcase and strode from the room.

Polly's heart sank. What a mess she had got herself into. Not only did she find her new boss extremely attractive, she had angered him and possibly jeopardised Green Lives' contract by her stupidity. How would she stand a journey to London sitting next to him?

3

The protest march at Croombs Wood turned out to be a social occasion. Polly had driven north from the city for an hour towards the edge of her home village. She parked in a layby and crunched her away along a gravel path which wound its way from the side of the road, through the threatened wood, and came out into a grassy glade. The glade was thronging with local people and their chatter had sent the birds scattering into the sky.

Polly spied her mother, dressed in a bright crimson raincoat, laughing with her 'lunching friends', Mel and Isla. She threaded her way through the people, nodding and waving to acquaintances. She had grown up in the village and knew most of them.

'Oh, here she is. Polly!' Her mother waved frantically. 'Come and join us.

We're about to march.'

'Hello, Mum, Mel, Isla.' Polly grinned. 'Where are the pitchforks?'

'Don't be silly, dear. It's a peaceful march. We've invited the local press and Isla's going to be interviewed on the radio. Have you seen your father?'

'Probably hiding from the noise, like the wildlife.'

'See if you can find him, there's a dear. Once the march is over, will you come and have lunch with us? I've invited our new neighbour.'

'Someone's bought the farm?' Polly asked, intrigued. Claxton Farm had lain empty for years. It was still in good repair, but the owner lived in Australia and had never visited it. Polly's mother and father owned the neighbouring house a few miles away, separated from the farm by a few neglected fields and overgrown hedgerows.

'They've rented it for six months. Still, it'll be lovely to have some company. I can see a few dinner parties in the near future.'

'I hope they enjoy partying,' said Polly wryly. Once her mother got under way with a social calendar, it was time to beware.

A tall, lean figure, stooping slightly, emerged from the trees. His face lit up when he saw Polly.

'Dad! It's good to see you.' Polly gave her father a hug. 'Find any good birds in there?'

Mr Baker shook his head and wiped the lenses of his binoculars. 'No birds, but plenty of people milling about. It'll be nice when this is over.'

There was a shout from the end of the glade. The protest march had begun. Polly and her father caught up with her mother and walked briskly through the trees. The air smelt sweet with the promises of spring; everywhere buds were bursting open and wild garlic and bluebells were breaking out of the rich soil. *It is heaven*, thought Polly. *Why would anyone want to destroy it to make a road?*

Unbidden, an image of Jake Grayling

sprang into her mind. She could not imagine him in a million years on a protest march, but she could easily picture him in a hard hat, giving orders to lay the Tarmac over the wood. His words from yesterday's meeting rang in her head. *We build houses; that's how we make our money.*

She felt angry just remembering it. He was like a block of stone which would not budge. He had been quite cold in his manner to her, just because she'd spoken her mind. Well, the fight wasn't over yet. She would save Monmeir, whether he liked it or not.

★　★　★

An old green Land Rover was parked in front of her parents' house. Polly drove past it, frowning. Presumably this belonged to the new neighbouring farm tenant. She left her car tucked under the rhododendron bushes at a jaunty angle. Her parents had arrived behind her, and a tall figure unfolded itself

37

from the Land Rover to greet them.

Polly gasped. It looked like . . . it couldn't be! But it was — Jake Grayling. He was dressed casually in faded jeans and a black sweatshirt but this only served to accentuate his broad shoulders and muscled thighs. Polly looked away uncomfortably. Really, what was she doing? — practically devouring him with her gaze.

'What are you doing here?' she asked, tilting her chin, determined not to let him see his effect on her.

'Having lunch, I hope,' he replied lightly.

'Mr Grayling is our new neighbour at Claxton,' said Mrs Baker, puzzled by Polly's reaction to their guest.

'Polly and I have already met,' confessed Jake with a grin. He took in Polly's clenched jaw, flashing emerald eyes and burnished curls. *What a strange little thing she is*, he thought. It was as if she was squaring up for a fight. Her cheeks were flushed, either from their march or from some

38

emotion, and her lips were surprisingly full and red. Jake had the most unsettling desire, for a swift second, to lean forward and kiss her on those tempting lips and take away her frown.

'Well, we'd love to hear all about it,' said her father cheerfully, ushering them into the warm hall.

Polly could hear the murmurs of her father and Jake in the living room as she helped her mother to heat the soup and lay out crusty bread and salads. She strained to hear what they were saying but could only make out their deep tones. Exasperated, she laid the table very quickly, then smoothed her hair and replaced her hair clasp.

'Like that, is it?' her mother said wickedly. 'You don't usually take the time to sort your hair.'

'Don't be silly, Mum,' Polly said sharply. 'He's our client, so I do have to project a neat appearance.'

She ignored her mother's smirk and went to call the men for lunch.

They were standing by the fireplace,

admiring a painting which hung dark and brooding — a large canvas which filled the wall with its beauty. The scene was of An Teallach, a high mountain in the north of Scotland.

'My father would have loved this,' Jake was saying.

'Was he an art lover, or a wilderness lover?' Mr Baker asked.

'Both, I suppose. He loved to roam the hills. When I was a small boy he would take me with him. I learned a considerable amount about nature and survival skills from him.'

'You were very fond of him.' It was a statement from Mr Baker, not a question.

'It's a pity your father isn't dealing with the Monmeir Loch development,' cut in Polly sarcastically. 'I might have a better chance of persuading him to keep it, than trying to convince you.'

Jake's expression went blank. 'I wish he could be here, too. Sadly he died when I was young,' he said stiffly.

Polly's father shot her a look which

said clearly that she had gone too far. She didn't need his reproof.

'Oh Jake. I'm so sorry. If I could eat my words, I would.' She was so distressed at her own tactlessness that impulsively she touched his hand to comfort him. The electric shock of that touch sent a shiver down her spine, and suddenly comfort was the last thing on her mind. Her blood sang with the need to touch him again, to hold him close and to taste his lips with her kiss. Polly took a step back. Surely Jake had noticed it too.

But if he had, he showed no sign of it. Instead he nodded his acknowledgement of her apology and followed Mr Baker's gesture towards the dining room table, where Polly's mother hovered with a tray of serving spoons and plates of steaming soup.

'Have you followed in your father's footsteps?' asked Mr Baker, curiously. He had immediately taken to this tall fellow with his quiet, confident ways, and wished that Polly had not taken such a dislike to him.

'No. I grew up in London with my mother, after my father died. I have followed in my mother's footsteps instead.'

'And what does she do?' enquired Mrs Baker, offering around home-made bread. *The boy has a good appetite*, she thought with satisfaction.

'She runs a media empire; very successfully as it turns out.'

'You say you've followed in her footsteps, but I don't see how a media empire and a property developer are the same,' Polly said.

'Yes you do, Polly. You said it yourself. *Everything with me is about money*. Remember?'

His tone was quiet. For once, Polly had no answer. She could only stare dumbly at him.

'Why don't you take Jake to see the viewpoint?' Mrs Baker said brightly, to fill the awkward silence. Really, her younger daughter could be quite exasperating sometimes. Did she have to alienate the first attractive young man she had met in a long time?

'I'd like to see it,' said Jake politely.

And so Polly found herself taking him on the long, winding path behind the house which led to a rock face and hillside. She walked briskly, annoyed with her mother for suggesting the outing. Her attraction to Jake was illogical and not worth pursuing. He quite clearly was not interested in her, never mind the fact that they were so obviously different from each other in their outlook and lifestyle. Polly walked faster, and Jake adjusted his long-legged stride to match her speed with ease. Polly began to feel out of breath. With irritation, she glanced at Jake to see that he looked relaxed and not in the least exerted.

'Shall we slow down?' he asked. 'You seem a little puffed.'

'I'm fine,' Polly returned grimly. She strode on and missed seeing the twitch of his lip indicating his enjoyment of teasing her.

The viewpoint was marked by a stone cairn right at the summit of the hill. To get there required a scramble up some scree onto a shale path with a couple of tricky steps to the top. Jake followed Polly as she nimbly sidestepped some falling pebbles from the scree and reached the path. She took her time now, carefully placing each foot so as not to slide from the slippery stones. Near the top she had to use both hands and feet, placing them in crevices to lift herself onto the ridge path to the summit.

Jake watched her. Suddenly he thought of Nina. He could never imagine her scrambling like this, outdoors. She was a hothouse species and would probably lack the nerve as well. He was uncomfortably aware how disloyal that sounded. He blocked out the vision of vivacious Polly, red hair flying in the breeze, lips pursed in concentration, and replaced it mentally with an image of Nina, ice-cool and beautiful in a cocktail gown, sipping champagne, as he had last seen her.

Polly's shout shattered Nina's image into a thousand pieces. Jake looked up at her, startled.

'Hurry up!' she yelled over the sound of the air soughing against the rock. 'It's stunning up here.'

Jake climbed up to join her. The late afternoon light was soft and dove-grey. It caught the silhouettes of the distant mountains and turned them purple and blue. The fields and hedges below them seemed unnaturally apple-green and almost fluorescent as they reflected the remains of the sun's rays. Polly took a deep breath of the fresh air, letting it fill her lungs, and felt the stress of the last few weeks drift away. She turned to talk to Jake and found him staring at her. He smiled and she found herself smiling back, looking into his dark blue eyes and seeing there a reflection of her own contentment with the moment.

'Your father would have liked this, from what you said,' Polly said softly.

Jake nodded. 'In this, I am my father's son.'

'It must be quite a contrast from your life in London.'

'And a blessed relief,' he said without thinking.

'Oh? Why is that?'

But Jake had turned away from her, straightening the collar of his coat and pulling his shoulders back firmly. Polly realised that she would not get an answer.

'I had better get back,' he said brusquely. 'There are papers I have to look at before we go to London on Monday.'

'I hope we don't get bored with each other on the flight,' Polly said cheerfully, hoping to break his suddenly sombre mood.

'It's a very quick flight and there won't be time to chat. Bring your laptop and papers so you can prepare for the meeting with Mr Rathbone.'

Polly made a face to his back as she followed him off the hill and back down the treacherous trail to her parents' house. Just when she felt she was getting to know him, he had reverted to being her none-too-friendly boss!

The trip to London would be interesting. Seeing him in his natural habitat was bound to be an eye-opener.

4

The journey to London was uneventful. Polly met Jake on the shuttle aeroplane at an outrageously early time of the morning. He was cool and smart in a grey suit, charcoal tie and crisp white shirt. Her heart did a little flip on seeing him. The corporate look was growing on her, she had to admit. Jake already had his laptop open and was working away in quiet concentration.

Polly sank into the seat opposite, glad of a rest. The Sunday spent with Laura had been exhausting. The little girl had had the most awful tantrums and Polly had been at her wits' end trying to calm her down without pandering to her demands. She was beginning to see why Lou was so tired all the time, if that was the way Laura behaved every day. No wonder Ian wanted a break from it all — it was just a pity he didn't seem to realise that Lou needed one just as much, or even more, than he did.

London was as noisy, crammed and hectic as Polly remembered it. They hurtled from plane to train to Tube and finally arrived at the revolving door and gleaming metal construction that was the Grayling Media Empire.

Jake turned to her. He had become more remote as the journey proceeded south, and now spoke in a clipped, formal way as if they had only just met. 'I have arranged to meet my mother for lunch. You have a choice. You are very welcome to join us, and we can then head directly to the design meeting. Or you may wish to look around London and meet me at Rathbone's.'

Polly had been looking forward to a chance to wander around the markets, looking for bargains, but she found herself saying, 'I'd love to join you.' The words were out before her brain had begun to think it through. What would Jake's mother think of her joining them? Presumably she would want time

49

alone with her only son. Curiosity wasn't enough to justify it, Polly thought guiltily. She looked at Jake's stony expression.

'Sorry,' she said, 'it was rude of me to intrude. Look, you go ahead and see your mum. I'm sure you will want time on your own, the two of you.'

Jake's mouth twisted ironically. He tried to imagine Shanna Grayling's expression if he was ever to call her 'Mum'.

'Actually, I think I'd prefer some company.' His jaw tightened and the stony look returned as he looked up at the vast office block. He took Polly's arm to guide her in through the swing door.

The Grayling Media Empire was on the fourteenth floor. They took the elevator in silence and stepped out onto plush carpeting, to be met by a wall of polished oak reception desk. The girl behind the desk recognised Jake and buzzed through to Mrs Grayling's office immediately.

'Darling, how wonderful to see you,' purred a rich voice with just a hint of an accent. Devon or Dorset, perhaps, Polly thought, but well ironed out by time or elocution lessons.

'Shanna.' Jake stooped to kiss her on both cheeks. 'How are you? This is my colleague, Polly Baker.'

He drew Polly closer. Polly wished she could block that jolt of electricity that shot through her with his every touch. Surely it was visible!

Mrs Grayling was tall and slender with ash-blonde hair that had been beautifully straightened and styled, making her seem youthful. Only the skin on her hands gave her away, with raised veins and a few darker patches of pigment. Polly put her in her sixties. Her eyes were dark blue like her son's and like Jake's, her gaze seemed to penetrate right through to Polly's core.

She took in Polly's ruffled curls, her scattering of freckles and her plain shoes and dismissed her as unimportant. *Probably a clerk or secretary*, her

51

expression said, *and not a very attractive one at that.*

Ignoring her completely after a cool 'How do you do?', she took Jake's hand and pulled him over to her office.

Polly followed them uncertainly, feeling like a puppy that had disgraced itself and was now unwanted. She tried to fix her hair back into its clasp but the chignon style had been a disaster which she would try to remember not to repeat. Suddenly a surge of anger washed over her. She might not be model material or have straight hair that behaved itself, but underneath it all she was an interesting person with views and opinions and deserved to be at least taken notice of.

Boosted by this thought, Polly stood a little taller and marched purposefully into the vast room where Jake and his mother were ensconced in two of the huge leather armchairs surrounding a glass-topped coffee table which could easily have served afternoon tea for a score of guests.

'When are you going to give up that ghastly business with Uncle Raymond and come and join me at Grayling Media?' Shanna was asking.

Jake grimaced. 'Let's not have that conversation again. You know where my interests lie.'

'Working in some awful out-of-the-way place providing little boxes for people to live in. Where's the fun in that? Here, you could become a household name. Join me on the board of directors, and name your price.' Mrs Grayling leaned back into the leather, managing not to crush her hair while doing so.

'People need affordable housing.'

'People also need green spaces,' Polly could not help adding.

Jake gave an exasperated sigh and glanced at each of them. Polly wanted to laugh. He had a hunted look. Then he saw her grin and shook his head, smiling.

'Polly is our very own ecologist,' he told Mrs Grayling.

She wrinkled her small, perfect nose as if there was a bad smell. 'Really, how interesting. I was under the impression that meant wearing tie-dyed skirts and nose rings while hugging trees.'

'Only on Tuesdays,' replied Polly, deadpan.

Mrs Grayling looked startled for a moment. Collecting herself, she focused on her son. 'Nina will be joining us for lunch. She has a shoot in the afternoon for that chocolate advert.'

'Perhaps we should get going, then,' Jake said, tightening the knot of his tie and buttoning his jacket. His expression was closed. *Who is Nina?* Polly wondered. Obviously someone Mrs Grayling approved of, judging by the warmth of her tone.

★ ★ ★

They lunched at Kizzy's. Polly recognised two familiar faces, actors from a TV series. It was clearly the 'in' place to be seen. There was a buzz in the air of excited voices and laughter, but it sounded stilted to Polly, as if Kizzy's itself was a film set and all the customers were acting out.

A tall young woman sat at a table near the back. As they approached she unfolded herself gracefully and stood up to greet them. Nina was exquisite. Her lemon-pale hair drifted becomingly around her heart-shaped face with its large grey eyes framed by thick, black lashes. She wrapped herself around Jake. Polly could smell her delicate flower fragrance, which was expensively sweet.

'I thought you were in Rome,' Jake said.

'I got back this morning. Shanna invited me for lunch, and once I knew you would be here, how could I resist?'

Jake kissed her lightly on the lips before turning politely to introduce Polly. Nina held out her hand. Polly took her cold, limp fingers. She had a sudden urge to crush them savagely, and became aware of a sudden hollowness in her chest. What had she been thinking? She knew Jake's reputation from Harriet's gossip. Did she really think that a man as gorgeous as Jake would have no constant girlfriend? That she, Polly, could waltz in and enthrall him? *Dream on*, Polly thought bitterly. No-one could compete with Nina's perfection. She and Jake were well suited — both entirely out of Polly's league!

'Ah yes,' Nina said, 'Jake told me about your campaign to save a pond. Take my advice; don't try to argue with him. He hasn't lost a deal yet.'

'Oh, he's young, there is still time,' returned Polly lightly, pasting a smile onto drawn lips.

'Let's eat,' Mrs Grayling said, gesturing to a passing waiter who responded immediately.

Polly's appetite had vanished. She pushed her food around the plate, listening to the others chat. It was another superficial world of high-profile models, photo shoots and celebrity gossip. With a pang, she wished to be at home again, eating at her parents' comfortable oak table, surrounded by people she truly cared about and only a step away from the many glories of the countryside.

She looked up and caught a look of concern in Jake's eyes. Nina glanced over at them and a flash of some dark emotion passed over her face. She nestled in to Jake's shoulder and took his hand.

'Darling, I meant to say that the shoot will be finished in a couple of days. Why don't I fly up and visit you after that? I would love to see the farm.'

Jake raised his eyebrows. 'I'd love that, Nina. I didn't ask you because I know how much you dislike the outdoors.'

'Only make sure you both return in time for the Mayor's Charity Ball,' admonished Mrs Grayling. 'Grayling Media and Rathbone's are both invited and it will certainly get good press coverage.'

Nina nodded enthusiastically. 'I have already bought my dress. When I walk up the red carpet I expect to get some really good images taken and hopefully get more work out of it.'

'You should come to the Ball, too,' Jake said unexpectedly to Polly.

She shook her head, confused. 'It's not really my cup of tea.'

'Nonsense,' said Nina, her eyes narrowing with amusement. 'You will enjoy it, trust me.'

She looked like the cat that had eaten the canary. Aware that she occupied the position of canary, Polly decided not to trust her.

'It will give Green Lives Consultancy good exposure. Neil will want you to take this opportunity,' said Jake firmly, as if it was settled.

'Polly and I must leave now,' he added, looking at his watch. Polly slipped on her coat and saw a fleeting look of displeasure on Nina's face as Jake kissed her cheek briefly and followed Polly to the door of the restaurant, promising his mother to write and call more frequently.

'Nina is lovely,' Polly said brightly as she hurried alongside him down the busy street.

'She is beautiful,' he agreed, 'and my mother is very fond of her.' He said no more and Polly was silent, too. They didn't sound like the words of a lover, but who could tell? Polly had never been good at reading the signs, hence her dreadful track record of disastrous relationships. *Not that there have been many*, she admitted to herself. Plump redheads with attitude were not in great demand in her neck of the woods.

★   ★   ★

Raymond Rathbone's office was in a tall building which appeared to be made entirely of steel and polished glass. The reception area was glossy with white marble and a fountain played in the centre, surrounded by green foliage. Polly felt dwarfed by it but Jake looked cool and confident, as if he were in his natural element. He guided Polly to the elevators and they stood in silence as they rose majestically to the tenth floor.

As the light flashed and the doors opened, Jake turned to her, his tone hesitant. 'You haven't met my uncle, have you?'

Polly shook her head 'He did visit Monmeir but I was away at a seminar. After that, I dealt with the project only through Neil.'

'He can be somewhat abrupt in his manner — and he's old-fashioned when it comes to women.'

'To translate — that means he doesn't approve of professional women?'

'You may need to persuade him otherwise.'

'He sounds charming.'

'He is a charming fellow once you get to know him.' Jake gave her an apologetic grin.

Polly gripped her bag firmly. Raymond Rathbone sounded awful, but there was no way he was going to intimidate her.

They followed a secretary into a huge room crammed with thick carpet, soft rugs and dark wood furniture.

Polly had barely sunk into her chair when a voice boomed, 'Ah, my dear boy, you made it!'

Raymond Rathbone was short and round and looked like a jolly Father Christmas, complete with a white beard and red, button nose. He wore a tweed jacket and mustard-yellow cravat, which sat oddly with his dark trousers and black shoes. He looked completely recovered from whatever illness he had suffered.

'And this must be Polly.' His handshake was crushing but Polly did not wince and merely returned the pressure. His eyebrows rose like little clouds and his eyes really twinkled.

'Well, well,' he boomed. 'Let us hear how you are running my business north of the border. Katie, bring us coffee and cakes, there's a good girl.'

Katie, a pale whippet of a girl, almost ran out of the room at his bidding. She looked terrified of him.

Polly listened while Jake talked his uncle through the various plans and maps and the legalities of the development. There were other projects, too, which Jake was in charge of and Polly was surprised to find out just how large the company was and how much responsibility Jake had. It did not seem to faze him, and Polly's impression was that business was going well.

'There is potential for more housing if you fill in that area over there,' Rathbone said, jabbing a stout finger towards the outline of the loch.

'You can't do that!' protested Polly. 'There are protected species living in the habitats there.'

'We certainly *can* do that.' Rathbone's voice rose. 'If we have to move some wildlife for publicity reasons, so be it, but that land is valuable.'

'I quite agree with you,' Polly said calmly. Rathbone and Jake stared at her, one with a furious expression, one with a pained look of anticipation.

'Yes, it is valuable,' she continued. 'For its natural resources.'

She opened her bag and drew out a large map which she spread out over the top of their plans and papers.

Eagerly now, Polly bent over the table and jabbed with her own finger while explaining how attractive the housing could be, edging the loch, and how people would love to have a local nature reserve right on their doorstep.

Jake watched her. Her face was prettily flushed and animated, her green eyes flashing. Her burnished hair was tumbling unheeded down her back. Suddenly he wanted to take her and kiss those red lips and feel her passion directed towards him. How had he ever thought her plain?

He stood, shocked by his thoughts. They did not fit into his carefully planned future. He must think of the business, and his duties to his mother and family.

When Polly had finished her speech, she stood back. Jake was looking at her strangely. She smiled in an attempt to encourage a response and some support from him. Still he said nothing. Polly frowned at him impatiently and nodded towards her map.

A great roar of laughter startled them both. Raymond Rathbone thumped her on the shoulder.

'Brilliant — a young lady who knows what she wants and how to get it.'

Katie, who had tiptoed in and laid a tray on the table, shrank back at this. She edged round the room and escaped.

'Jacob, my boy, you should ditch that Tina and marry this girl instead. She has a fine head on her shoulders and knows how to argue her case.'

'It's Nina, Uncle, not Tina, as you know perfectly well. And as we are simply good friends, I am in no danger of marrying her. That reminds me — she is coming up to Claxton Farm at the weekend, so will you please make an attempt to be civil?'

Polly's heart lightened. So he and Nina were not lovers after all.

Rathbone winked at Polly. 'I am looking forward to my visit and will make every effort to be interested in dieting and cosmetics and dresses. Perhaps Polly can take us on a tour of the loch while we are up. That will give me an excuse to get away.'

Polly hid a smile. Rathbone was clearly an old rascal, but she was warming to him.

Then Jake's next words turned her to ice.

'My next step is to get a hydrologist in. I think you are right, Uncle — we are wasting space for houses if we don't drain the loch. Polly, when we get back, your job is to report on how we can move the animals and plants and anything else we have to, to comply with regulations.'

'Did you not hear a word I said?' she said, aghast.

'Please prepare your report as requested,'

Jake said abruptly. His face was closed and his jaw set. No-one could have guessed the battle that was raging within him. He was furious with himself for even thinking about kissing Polly Baker; furious at his own disloyalty to the game plan, forgetting his duty to his mother and his future. Annoyed, too, at Raymond for pretending he thought Jake and Nina were still together, and for remarks about marriage that echoed uncomfortably close to his own inner voice.

★　　★　　★

The journey home was spent apart. The cabin was teeming with people heading north. Polly deliberately sat where the other seats were all taken. Jake took himself off to the next available space. Polly could see a woman move her bags to make room for him, flicking her long hair back. She burned with jealousy. *Don't be silly*, she told herself angrily, *he's not for me. He is the enemy now.*

Everything I hold dear, he despises. There is no way we can ever agree on any of these important issues.

In the airport she pointedly ignored him during the seemingly endless wait for their bags on the carousel. He did not try to speak to her, but seemed to be in a world of his own, his brows drawn.

Her mobile phone rang. It was Lou.

'Oh, Polly, please say you'll come and help me. Ian has left me.' Lou was crying hopelessly.

'What do you mean? Is he coming back?'

'No. He can't take it any more. Oh, Polly, what will I do?'

Polly glanced at her watch. It was nine o'clock at night. She still had reports to type up from the day's meeting and she was dying for a shower and a glass of wine, to unwind and think over a day which had been full of confused emotions. But helping Lou was more important.

'Lou, I'll come straight from the

airport. Don't worry. It will be okay, I'll sort it out.'

Digesting the news, Polly's heart sank. This would devastate Lou, and her parents too. They had always been a very close family and Ian was a big part of that. Should they tell their parents now, or hope that Ian would come to his senses and return quickly? Polly closed her eyes and tried to think. Life had become horribly complicated by Lou's problems — and especially because of Jacob Grayling and his appalling, uncompromising edicts.

5

Even before Lou opened the door, Polly could hear chaos. Laura was screaming without pause for breath and Lou was shouting. Something thudded heavily against the front door, then it opened and a flustered Lou stood there, hair sticking up as if she had had an electric shock.

'Thank goodness you're here,' Lou said, pulling Polly inside hurriedly and slamming the door as another missile hit it. 'Laura, *stop* that!'

The screaming intensified and a small, red-faced child appeared at the bottom of the stairs.

'Aunty Polly's here,' said her mother desperately, before bursting into tears herself.

Polly fought the urge to cover her ears and run from the house. Instead she scrabbled in her handbag and found an old packet of tissues, rather grubby-edged but unused. She wiped Laura's nose and hugged her close until the little body stopped heaving and her crying calmed to hot, ragged breaths against Polly's neck.

'Want Teddy,' Laura said, between hiccups.

'Tell me where Teddy is and we'll go together and get him,' Polly said gently, stroking her niece's warm head.

'Mummy took him away.' The tears were starting up again.

Lou looked guilty. 'You were naughty, Laura, that's why Mummy put Teddy in the cupboard.'

Polly lifted Laura. 'Now that you are going to be good, I'm sure Mummy will give Teddy back.' She gave her sister a look of disapproval. Lou's face crumpled. She stumbled up the stairs and a few minutes later she was back with a moth-eaten teddy bear.

Laura grabbed it happily and burrowed into its fat belly.

'Want to help me to do a jigsaw?'

Polly carried Laura and Teddy into the living room. Stepping over toys and pillows and plates of uneaten biscuits and browning apple pieces, she cleared a space and started to set out a fairy princess puzzle.

'Maybe Mummy would like to help while I make a pot of tea?'

Lou edged reluctantly into the room. Polly gave her a hug. Lou looked awful. She had a pale complexion naturally, but now there were dark circles under her eyes and her skin was blotchy from crying. Polly was fairly sure the tears had been cried over days, not hours.

It broke her heart to see Lou so wary of Laura. The little girl's tantrums must have become terrible since Ian left.

Polly clattered about in the kitchen, taking her time. She washed up mounds of dirty dishes, searched for a teapot and found some crushed teabags jammed into a coffee jar. She put the teapot and mismatching cups on a tray with a plate of softening biscuits. Better than nothing. The state of Lou's kitchen made her realise that her sister had not been coping for some time. The old Lou, the Lou who was in control of her life, had had a house that was gleaming, tidy and spotlessly clean. Laura had been much calmer then, too. What had happened to make everything slide so?

The phone rang as Polly handed Lou a cup of tea. Clutching the cup like a lifeline, Lou picked up the receiver. It was Ian.

'Where are you?' she cried.

'It doesn't matter,' he replied. 'I just need some time away, to think.'

'What about me? When do I get some time away, ever?'

'Let's not start this again, Lou,' he said wearily. 'It's not about who's right or wrong. I . . . I just need to sort myself out.'

'Laura misses you.'

'And I miss her too.'

'So come home.' Lou's knuckles were white against the phone cord.

'I . . . I can't. I'll ring you tomorrow.'

There was an abrupt click as the line went dead.

Lou bit her bottom lip. She looked at Polly, eyes huge. Polly, having picked up the gist of the conversation, was bubbling with suppressed anger at Ian. How selfish could he be! Here were Lou and little Laura, clearly struggling to cope and miserable, and Ian was off somewhere quiet to 'sort himself out'!

Lou rubbed her arms as if she was cold. 'I hope he's all right, 'she said wretchedly. 'I worry about him, all on his own with his thoughts.'

Polly felt a shaft of shame pierce her. This was real love. While she was thinking bad thoughts about her brother-in-law, in spite of his actions his wife still put his welfare before everything.

'He'll come home when he's ready,' she offered, hugging her sister.

Lou shook her head. 'I don't know if he will.'

Polly was chilled. Suddenly she was the one needing reassurance. 'He loves you, Lou. He loves Laura. How can he stay away?'

'Love is complicated, Polly,' sighed Lou. 'One day you'll understand.'

'Last bit, last bit, Mummy,' shouted Laura triumphantly, waving a lurid pink piece of jigsaw at them.

'Great! Let's do another one.'

Lou settled herself on the floor beside Laura, armed with a stack of jigsaw boxes, while Polly poured more tea.

Her mobile buzzed in her handbag. Excusing herself, Polly went into the hall to answer it, assuming it would be a work call.

A deep voice spoke. It was Jake. 'I wondered if you were okay. You looked preoccupied when you left the airport.'

The leap of her heart, that frisson of excitement from hearing his voice and some other emotion that Polly did not want to examine, annoyed her. She was still angry with him anyway about his dictates from the meeting. Neatly ignoring the fact that he was her boss and could dictate anything he liked, Polly let her anger soar.

'Why do you care?' she asked rudely, 'Of course I was preoccupied, after you decided to drain the loch in spite of my professional advice.'

There! That would put him in his place.

'It's more than that, isn't it? You looked concerned, as if something bad had happened. I was worried about you.'

Her mind might want to stay angry, but her heart had other ideas. It was overjoyed to know that Jake had been thinking about her.

'A few problems at home. It won't affect my work,' she said stiffly.

'About the loch — ' Jake started to say.

'How could you do that?' Polly burst out. 'Decide to drain it, making a snap decision? It's — it's — awful!'

'I have a duty to the company. We build houses. By draining the loch, we will be able to fit more onto the site.'

'Does duty come before everything else? What about doing what's *right?* What about your gut instinct?'

'Duty is a promise, is it not? If I run from my duty, it's a betrayal of trust.' His voice was serious.

'What if the duty is wrong? What if your instinct is telling you the truth?' Polly's voice was impassioned as she imagined the beauty of Monmeir Loch gone forever.

'I have duties to my family, Polly, whatever my instinct and my heart may tell me.' He gave a strangled sigh.

His heart? Since when had his heart become involved in the project? Were they talking about the same thing?

'I can't tell you what to do, Jake,' Polly said harshly. 'Only you can make the decision, but if it's the wrong one then you will have to live with the consequences.'

'I know that, Polly,' he groaned, 'but what is better? Pleasing myself at everyone else's expense, or doing the right thing and at least having the satisfaction of that?'

Polly had no idea now what he was alluding to. Following his train of thought was likely to take her to places she did not want to visit, so she decided to keep it simple.

'Revoke your decision on drainage,' she challenged.

He paused as if clearing his head. 'I can't. It's in the minutes of meeting. It still may be the best solution.'

'Then there's no more to discuss,' Polly said abruptly, her anger returning. She pressed the button to end the call, and stomped back into the living room.

'Of all the insufferable men!' Polly shook her fists, making Laura giggle and raise her own tiny hands in mimicry.

'Is there some sort of problem with your work?' asked Lou in concern.

Polly related the conversation she had had with Jake, her voice snappy with irritation. Lou was puzzled.

'He sounds lovely — there aren't many bosses who would phone to check on your welfare like that.'

Polly snorted rudely. 'He doesn't really care. He just wants to make sure I put in that report for his hydrologist. The nerve of the man.'

Lou's eyes widened and she stared at her sister. Suddenly she burst out laughing wildly, and clapped her hands.

'Methinks the lady doth protest too much.'

'What are you talking about?' said Polly uneasily.

Perhaps Lou was hysterical. First tears, now uncontrollable laughter. Was she losing her grip altogether? Lou grabbed her and pulled her closer.

'It sounds to me as if you are in love with your mysterious boss!'

'Don't be ridic . . . ' The words faltered from Polly's lips as she realised that Lou was absolutely right.

Somehow he had got under her skin. In spite of the fact that his viewpoint on life was completely and utterly contrary to hers and that he had a lifestyle she could never fit into, Polly had fallen for him. And fallen hard. Even the sound of his name made her heart soar. He may infuriate her mind, but her body knew better.

Polly groaned. She flung herself onto the sofa.

'There's no future in loving Jake,' she said quietly. 'He has a gorgeous female friend, Nina, who is perfect for him and bent on being Mrs Grayling. She will make a wonderful hostess for business dinners and entertaining. He also has a dragon of a mother determined that he will work for her high profile media empire. He is out of my league.'

'On the other hand,' replied Lou, 'he's as yet unmarried, works very successfully for himself and appears to enjoy walking in the countryside with defeatist redheads!'

'Ah, you've been talking to Mum. She's such a terrible gossip.'

'Which can be useful at times like these. It's not like you, Polly, to give up without a fight. The more the odds are stacked against you, the harder you usually attack.'

'On behalf of wildlife. That's a little different. My track record with relationships is laughably poor.'

'You have many fine qualities,' said Lou firmly. 'And if Jake can't see that, he isn't worth the bother.'

'Thanks, big sister,' Polly grinned. 'I'll send Jake over so you can tell him.' But, strangely, she did feel better for the pep talk. At the end of the project Jake would return to London and she would most likely never see him again, but for the next few months he was her boss and he was here. Polly could only hope that would be sufficient consolation for her heart.

6

The week passed in a blur. Polly kept her head down and worked hard, avoiding Jake whenever he was in the office. It helped that he did not seek her out. In fact he appeared to be keeping away from her too.

The team was busy. A new contract had been taken on and Neil had started allocating surveys and mapping tasks. Even Harriet had been roped in to walking transects and capturing insects, as time was tight and Neil and Polly had other things to prioritise. Polly found herself snowed under with plotting graphs, finding out land owner- ship details and one hundred and one other jobs outside of the Monmeir project. Reluctantly she had researched the legal requirements for moving great crested newts and rare plants and the best practice for transferring these species to other areas of habitat. It made her want to scream at Jacob Grayling for his obstinacy. If only she had been more persuasive with her plans for a nature reserve! Unless there was a miracle, it would all go to ruin.

Thank goodness it was now the weekend. Much as she loved her job, Polly had not enjoyed explaining to Neil Jake's decision regarding the loch and the urgent need to plan for translocation of species. She lay in bed listening to the birds singing outside, watching a shaft of light play on the faded pink flowers of the wallpaper in her childhood room. Polly sighed contentedly. She was glad she had driven up to her parents' house for the weekend. A smell of freshly brewed coffee wafted upstairs and she could hear the sizzle of bacon on her mother's ancient black skillet. Polly threw back the duvet and stretched, feeling the tension of the week drain away.

After a hearty breakfast Polly tugged on woollen socks and battered hillwalking boots. Slinging a rucksack of provisions over her shoulders and checking she had a compass and map, she set out across the fields towards Ben Dhubh. It was a small hill compared to the majestic mountains of the Highlands, yet high and craggy enough to give her a good physical workout. But as she put one boot in front of the other, watching the mosses compress and spring back as her feet passed, hearing herself breathe heavily as the exercise kicked in, Polly realised it was her heart and soul that needed a workout. How had Jake Grayling managed to unsettle her so completely? Blast the man! He had turned all her principles upside down.

Polly had always been very clear in her own mind about right and wrong. She had never subscribed to the view of the world in shades of grey. Black and white. It was simple. Anyone who didn't match up to her expectations was shunned. People frequently disappointed her with their vague views on topics that she felt very strongly about. Then, along came Jake Grayling. Distracting her with his strong frame and stunning good looks, making her dizzy with attraction. Damn it — making her fall in love with him! Polly crunched the stones angrily under the thick soles of her boots. Jake's views were the antithesis of hers. He wanted to destroy what she held dear.

Polly took a deep breath of the fresh, sweet air and looked around at the swaying grasses, soaring buzzards and the puffy clouds. How could anyone rather have brick and Tarmac instead of this? She heard Jake's voice in her head speaking about affordable housing, and how people deserved a decent place to live. He had spoken quite passionately about the subject at a conference held at Green Lives the day after their return from London. She had avoided him by leaving early, but his views had rung in her head over and over again as if the facts wanted to make themselves heard. It had made her uncomfortable. Even if she accepted what he said, it was irreconcilable with her own beliefs. Under normal circumstances, with anyone else, Polly would have thrown up her hands in disgust and vowed to cold-shoulder him. But her heart and body betrayed her.

For the first time in her life, Polly began to think of compromise. With her new realisation that she loved Jake, she knew she could never ignore him or give him up simply because of his beliefs. She *would* have to sacrifice her love — but only because he would be returning to his jet-setting London life. Her love would remain hidden; something to sustain her when he had gone.

Polly stood at the summit of Ben Dubh and let the breeze buffet her. She had a sudden, wild impulse to scream her exhilaration and frustration into the wind. Turning to walk down the other side of the hill, she meandered along the deer track that was just as good as a path and meant she could avoid the boggy ground and the snares of heather roots that made walking so tiresome. As she concentrated on the trail, eyes to the ground, a movement startled her. A tiny bird flew suddenly up out of the tussocky grass. Gently she parted the grasses and there, tucked neatly in the ground, was a perfect little nest made out of grass stems. Two tiny eggs lay there.

'What treasure have you found?' said a deep, familiar voice. Polly felt the heat rise to her face. It was him. She shouldn't be surprised; after all, she was walking on land belonging to Claxton Farm, and where else would Jake be at the weekend? *And if you are honest*, the little voice in her head said, *that's why you chose to hike here, isn't it*?

Jake knelt beside her, his shoulder brushing hers as he peered at the tiny nest. She felt a tingle where their bodies touched. His chestnut hair was unruly in the breeze. She felt an urge to run her fingers through it. She could see the dark stubble along his jawline and his curved and very kissable lips.

His lips twisted in amusement as he looked at her, and Polly quickly shifted her gaze back to the nest, her heart thudding.

'It's a Meadow Pipit,' she said faintly.

Jake nodded. 'Yes, that's right — I remember my father showing me one when I was a child.'

They turned to each other at the same time and Polly realised how close they were. She felt his breath warm on her face and gazed again at his lips.

'Polly,' he murmured, and suddenly he kissed her. His mouth was hot and urgent on hers. The kiss intensified and she gave herself to it entirely.

'Oh, Polly,' he groaned and stroked her tangled curls back from her flushed face. Her lips were red and full, bee-stung from his kiss, and her eyes wide and shining. Jake thought her the most desirable woman he had ever seen. He leaned towards her to taste those lips again.

The sound of horses' hooves thudding made them spring apart guiltily. Jake got quickly to his feet and turned to meet the riders. Polly was left kneeling in the grass by the tiny nest, stunned at what had happened.

There were three riders, and only one was smiling in greeting. Raymond Rathbone tipped his riding helmet and boomed, 'Polly Baker! What a delightful suprise.'

'You do realise you are trespassing?' came the icy tones of the next rider. Shanna Grayling stared coldly at Polly.

Nina was watching her also. The model's eyes glinted as she took in Polly's dishevelled appearance and flushed face. She flicked a sharp glance between Jake and Polly and her lovely face narrowed unattractively. Polly couldn't blame her. It felt to her as if Jake's kiss was branded on her skin for all to see.

Jake's voice was hard as he frowned at his mother. 'Don't be so ridiculous, Shanna. These are my fields and Polly can walk through them any time she wishes.'

Shanna Grayling's mouth thinned. *If looks could kill*, Polly thought, watching the two women, *I'd be long gone.*

'Your fields, my boy?' Raymond Rathbone asked, raising a bushy eyebrow. 'Sounds as if you intend to buy the place.'

'I might at that, Uncle. I haven't decided.'

Mrs Grayling gave a gasp of shock. 'Buying! You can't surely intend to live in this godforsaken place?'

Jake's gaze was shuttered. 'Nothing is definite.'

'I can't understand why you would buy it,' Nina said in a soft voice, 'You know I don't like the country. This is hundreds of miles from London. It isn't even convenient as a weekend retreat.' She looked distastefully around her at the wild fields and hedgerows and the distant crags and hills, and gave a dramatic shiver.

'Remember the game plan, Jacob,'

added his mother darkly.

Game plan? Polly wondered what grand scheme Jake had, and what part his mother had in it. Nina was obviously a major element, too. Polly was quite sure that she herself did not feature.

Beside her, she felt Jake bristle. His shoulders were taut, pulled back stiffly, and he stood ramrod tall. She felt the strength and height of him shadow her. She felt sheltered by him, protected and safe. But she was not safe. She was not his to cherish or protect. Still, she saw Jake's jaw was firm as he reined in his temper and moved to his mother's side, speaking with deliberate patience.

'How can I forget it, Shanna, when you are always there to remind me? You don't need to worry. Claxton is my business and will have no influence on how I conduct my other business.'

'The nearest I want to get to it is on a horse's back,' Nina interrupted petulantly. She swung her mount around and galloped away, her pale hair streaking out like white silk. Shanna gave her son a thunderous look, wheeled and galloped after her.

'Remarkable how well she rides,' said Rathbone mildly, a wicked sparkle in his eyes. 'She learned it for the part in that film — what was it called?'

'*Selby's Daughter*. Unfortunately she failed the audition,' replied Jake vaguely, his thoughts clearly elsewhere.

Polly wished she could ask him what they were. Was he regretting their kiss? Was he thinking of the game plan his mother had set out for him? Or was he simply upset that he and Nina had had a tiff? This last thought gave Polly an almost physical pain. Did he love Nina? If he did, why had he kissed Polly? Was she a mere distraction, a light flirtation to pass the time while he worked in the north?

Polly felt a headache push at her skull as the unwelcome thoughts circled in her head. Suddenly she had to get away. She picked up her rucksack and zipped her jacket.

'I must get back. I'm helping Mum paint the outhouse today.' She had offered to help, dreading the job, but now it was a welcome escape.

For a moment she thought Jake would stop her, but he let his arm sink to his side and kept his expression polite.

'We are visiting Monmeir Loch tomorrow,' said Rathbone. 'Join us.'

It was less an invitation than a command, but issued in a warm tone. Polly nodded, although she dreaded the emotional upheaval of being close to Jake again and prayed that Nina and Shanna Grayling would not wish to tramp about in marsh water.

Jake watched the small figure walking steadily away, curls bouncing against her rucksack. His mind was in turmoil. Why had he kissed Polly Baker? Of all the stupid . . . Yet how could he not! An image of her, passionate in his arms, threatened to overwhelm him entirely. He turned away resolutely. His uncle gave him a wicked grin. 'There's a rain shower coming, my boy. That'll cool you down.'

He waved cheerily and trotted off, leaving Jake to walk home alone.

★　★　★

Polly was covered in whitewash when the idea came to her. She startled her mother by waving the paintbrush in the air, thereby adding more white freckles to her face and hair. 'I've got it!'

'Got what? Insanity?' asked her mum, still painting furiously.

'The perfect compromise for the building plans at the loch!' exulted Polly.

Her mother stood still, paint dripping unheeded. 'That is the first time in your life I have ever heard you decide to compromise on anything. He really must be someone special.'

Polly blushed. Her mother laughed and hugged her affectionately.

Yes, it was a great idea. She couldn't wait to tell Jake.

★　★　★

Jake returned to the farmhouse, his mother's warning still singing in his ears. *The game plan*. He had first heard those words some ten or more years ago, when summoned by Shanna Graying to her office. Jake was newly qualified as an architect and had started working for Raymond Rathbone, on the shop floor as it were. Rathbone believed in working up the ladder and Jake agreed with him. Shanna had other ideas.

'It's ridiculous of Raymond. We both know he intends to make you his business partner. Why on earth are you working in that dreadful office with those . . . those *youths?*'

Jake had sighed. 'Uncle Raymond and I agree that it's the best way to learn the business. Start at the bottom and work gradually up. By the time I make partner, I'll be well versed in all aspects of Rathbone Developments.'

'You should give it up. There is a

place in Grayling Media waiting for you, one that will suit your status as my son. Why persist with this nonsense? I want the best for you, Jacob. You need a game plan.'

'Game plan?'

'Yes. You need to know what you are aiming for, ten years down the line. It is not enough to wander and dream and hope it will all work out. You are young now, but soon you will need a wife. I have in mind someone attractive and high-profile. A young woman who is accomplished and can accompany you to dinners and functions or equally well provide superb catering at home for when you entertain business connections.'

Jake laughed. 'Does such a paragon exist?'

'Don't mock. I know you have your girlfriends and equally I suspect your heart has never been involved. That's a good thing. Love just makes things messy. Think of your marriage as a business contract designed to improve your career. Now, do you remember Nina Chalmers?'

Jake had gone along with his mother's plans. He always went along with them to keep the peace. Although he was delaying joining her in the Grayling Media Empire, he knew that one day his business interests and hers would combine. It was simple. She was the only real family he had, other than Raymond. Nina was just another piece of the puzzle. They had gone out a few times before Jake had gently but firmly detached himself from her cloying attentions. Yes, she was beautiful and would make a model wife, but there was something essential missing from her. He didn't expect to love his wife, but his instinct told him that he could and should do better than Nina. Since then, however, she had remained friendly with Shanna, who still held out hope that they would get back together in time.

Jake remembered his mother's parting words.

'One day you will take on the mantle of the family business from me, Jacob. That's why you must always remember our game plan. I am depending upon you for that.'

Now, ten years later, he was still following it. There was no company wife. Shanna was still dangling Nina at him and he admitted he was almost ready to cave in and accept his fate. Then he had met Polly Baker. She had an unnerving effect on him. He could not stop thinking about her. She was a strange, infuriating mixture of vulnerability and fieriness and all he wanted to do was kiss her and kiss her until she melted into his arms and then never let her go.

Finally Jake Grayling was in love. With the most unsuitable girl he could ever offer up to his mother and the family game plan.

7

Lou arrived the next morning just as Polly was sorting out her binoculars, pond net and plant identification guides which she would need for the visit to Monmeir Loch. She could hear her mother's cry of delight from downstairs and the shrieks and giggles from Laura at seeing her granny. Polly shoved her things haphazardly into a large rucksack, ran a brush quickly through her hair and went downstairs, two at a time, to greet them.

'And how's Ian?' her mother was asking, still holding Laura in her arms.

Lou glanced briefly at Polly. 'He's still away on that business trip. It's been extended.'

'Goodness, it's taking a while,' remarked her mother mildly, tickling Laura's nose.

The little girl laughed.

'Actually I was hoping you could help,' said Lou awkwardly. 'I need someone to look after Laura today while I go up to town for a few things.'

'Can't today, love. Your Dad and I are visiting the Brooks. Mrs Brooks is in hospital and Jimmy isn't coping very well. I'm going to clean up the house for him, get some shopping in.'

'Polly?' said Lou desperately, turning to her sister with a look of hope.

'I'm working,' said Polly, shaking her head.

'On a Sunday?'

'I've been asked for a site visit by the boss, I can't really refuse.' *And I don't want to*, thought Polly, *if it means seeing Jake again*. However complicated that might be. She would have to be polite and distant. There could be no repeat of yesterday's kiss. Her cheeks burned at the memory. Polly would have to make it clear that yesterday had been an anomaly, a glitch, a moment of madness. She had no desire to be one of Jake's flings. Until she knew what was in his mind and what part Nina played in his famous game plan, she was determined to be reserved and in control.

Lou's wail brought her back to the present sharply.

'What am I going to do?' She grabbed Polly and took her aside as Mrs Baker sang to Laura and promised her a cookie in the kitchen.

'You've got to help me, Polly. I'm meeting up with Ian — it's our chance to put things right.'

'That is important. You two need time alone to talk. I can take Laura along to work. If Rathbone doesn't like it, tough.'

Confident words, but Polly hoped that Raymond Rathbone had a soft side to him and didn't sack her on the spot.

Monmeir Loch looked idyllic, a blue shiny mirror amongst soft tufts of grass, surrounded by bluebells and yellow primroses and white garlic flowers. It was a very different scene from Polly's last visit. She shuddered, remembering her narrow escape from drowning during the storm, and her timely rescue by Jake Grayling.

'Pretty flowers,' said Laura, pulling up some bluebells to make a posy.

She gave it to Polly, beaming. Polly looked at her little niece, standing in the mud with her bright red wellies and plastic raincoat, and felt a rush of love for her.

'Thank you, darling. Are you going to help Auntie Polly today?'

Laura nodded eagerly. Polly gave her a pond net.

'We'll start with snails and beetles. Let's see how many you can find.'

The rumble of a Land Rover made her turn. Jake parked the battered vehicle, waved to her and started walking towards them. Where was Rathbone? Where were Nina and Mrs Grayling? Polly's heart thumped loudly as he approached.

'Where's Mr Rathbone?'

'He'll join us as soon as he can. In the meantime you'll have to put up with just my company.'

'I expected some hardships with the job,' said Polly lightly, to hide her confusion and delight at seeing him again.

'Is it a hardship to spend time with me, Polly?' he asked, his voice deep and gravelly. His eyes were dark, fixed on her face.

She stepped back, even as her heart urged her on. He would kiss her. Polly could sense it. Suddenly Laura shrieked with excitement. Jake frowned as the tiny figure raced over to them, spraying water and weed from her net.

'I got one, I got one!'

Jake crouched down and peered into the net. A large, glistening water snail lay there.

'So you have,' he said. 'A king-sized one at that.'

Laura grinned proudly. Jake's quizzical look was for Polly. She took a deep breath.

'Laura's my niece. She's helping me today.'

She waited for his disapproval, for his reminder that she was being paid a good deal of money for her time today. Instead Jake held out a friendly hand to Laura.

'Have you heard of water boatmen?' he asked conversationally.

Laura shook her head.

'Well, let's see if we can find one.'

Polly left them to it, taking her time to sample vegetation in her survey areas, keying out difficult specimens in her handbook. She loved this kind of work, absorbed in tiny details which were quite clearly right or wrong with no shades of uncertainty, no doubts lurking in between. She looked over to the edge of the loch where all her shades of grey and all her doubts were centred in a tall, broad-shouldered man who was now in charge of pond net and jam jar while Laura scampered along ahead of him. Polly could hear her gleeful shouts and the deeper, even tones as Jake answered her patiently.

Polly shut her book and slung her

rucksack on her back. She had enough data to write her next report for Green Lives. She wandered through the long grass to join the others, smelling the pungent garlic leaves and the indefinable freshness of late spring bursting from the soil.

Jake and Laura were admiring tadpoles which were wriggling in the jar.

'Mr Rathbone hasn't turned up yet?' asked Polly.

Jake rose from his crouched position and glanced at her sheepishly.

'I don't think he'll turn up at all. I volunteered to come in his place to give him a rest. He's still not well.'

Polly felt her spirits soar. He wanted to be with her. Then she thought of Nina and how perfect she was for Jake, and her spirits sank; a rollercoaster of emotions which drained her energy and left her weak.

'Doesn't Nina mind you working on a Sunday?'

His expression closed. Polly wished

she had not mentioned the model.

'Nina and my Mother are flying back to London today. They miss the shops and the buzz of the big city.'

'I'm sorry. I know how much you wanted them to like Claxton Farm.'

'Given more time, I'm sure they will come to see its charm, as I have.'

Polly doubted that, but Jake's abrupt tone warned her to leave the subject alone.

'I'm hungry,' piped up Laura. Her bottom lip trembled as if she was ready to cry. Polly knew how swiftly crying could change to tantrums.

'Okay darling, let me find you a snack.' Polly searched her bag but had forgotten to pack any food. When she was working she was usually too absorbed to eat, and had overlooked the fact that small children need many, regular top-ups.

'Oh-oh. Looks like Auntie Polly is in trouble,' Jake whispered to Laura. 'Shall we help her out?'

Laura sniffed and nodded, holding

her tears back for now as curiosity got the better of her. Jake rummaged in his coat pocket and flourished a chocolate bar. Laura clapped her hands and took it from him hungrily.

Jake and Polly sat on a dry, flat stone outcrop and watched her eat.

'You're a complete natural with children,' Polly remarked thankfully. 'What's your secret?'

'I always remember how patient and kind my father was with me. I don't have many memories of him as I was still small when he died, but the memories I do have are full of love.'

'I can't imagine not having my dad or my mum. It must have been awful.'

'You are very lucky, Polly. From what I've seen of your parents, you have a strong, loving family. I envy you that.' Jake's voice was serious.

Polly thought of Lou and Ian. They had had a strong, loving bond for ten years, yet it was fraying until it appeared to be beyond repair.

She shivered. It had begun to rain, a

light drizzle which threatened to turn into something much heavier. Laura had finished her chocolate bar and was making mud pies at the edge of the loch. Her raincoat was rimmed with dark soil and her hands were completely black. She was singing a Christmas song to herself about Santa and his reindeer and the jolly hollydays, happily oblivious to the fact that it was spring and the promise of summer was on the horizon. Not that it felt like it in this weather.

Polly was on the point of calling to Laura and packing up to go home when Jake spoke.

'Perhaps Laura would like a visit to Claxton Farm before you go home. She can see the newborn lambs, and it would give you a chance to scrape some Monmeir mud off her before her mother sees her.'

Polly grinned. 'I was just wondering what Lou would do to me if I returned her daughter in her present state.'

She hesitated, kicking pebbles with

her boot. Was it wise to go to Jake's house? Were her feelings hidden sufficiently? She had to maintain a friendly distance from him. There had to be no inkling of her desire and her love for him. She looked up at him. Jake smiled back at her but his eyes were puzzled as he waited for an answer.

'That would be lovely,' Polly heard herself say. Before she could change her mind, she folded her wet pond net carefully, tucked the identification keys into her rucksack and made a mental note to type up her findings that evening. She called to Laura and they made their way through the soaking grasses and squelchy marsh to Jake's Land Rover.

★   ★   ★

'I have to confess I'm curious to see inside Claxton Farm again,' she told Jake as they drove along bumpy roads with the windscreen wipers now on full speed against the sheets of rain. The

108

interior of the vehicle was warming up with hot air blasting from the air vents and Polly could feel the chill disappearing from her bones. Laura's face was rosy red and she was busy drawing pictures on the steamy window; stick figures and pond creatures and unidentifiable swirls and zigzags. She kept up a running commentary as she drew, quite content for Polly and Jake to chat to her and over her at the same time.

'I didn't realise you knew the owner.'

'Mr Flanagan was a friend and neighbour of my parents. I was often sent over with casseroles and cakes, especially once he became rather infirm. My mum likes to keep everyone well-fed, as you experienced when you came for lunch. When he died, his son inherited the farm but as far as I know he has no intention of returning from Australia to live in it. It's been lying empty for some years.'

Polly cast her mind back to Claxton Farm in the days when she had visited as a teenager. Her memories were of a dark, old-fashioned farm kitchen smelling somewhat of old age, dust and damp. The hallway was stacked with newspapers and farming journals, rusty farm implements and bits of tractor engine that Mr Flanagan was tinkering with but never quite finished mending. It was very much the lair of an aged widower with no housekeeper. Polly had found it fascinating, and the old man had many tales to tell about the faded framed photographs of his ancestors that hung haphazardly around the farmhouse.

'I'm surprised you have lambs. I didn't think it was being run as a farm any more.'

'I bought the lambs,' Jake said, sounding embarrassed. He glanced over and gave her a self-deprecating grin. 'Although I'm only renting the place, I hope you will see a difference in it. It feels like a second home to me. I'm playing at farming, I'm afraid.'

'What will happen to the lambs when you leave?'

'And the chickens.'

Polly started to laugh because he sounded just like a child caught out in a naughty deed and confessing by degrees. Jake laughed too, and Laura joined in because they both sounded so happy. When he had dried his eyes, Jake said, 'I hope to buy Claxton and run it as a going concern.'

'An absentee landlord, you mean?' asked Polly.

'Possibly. I don't know.' Jake turned the Land Rover hard into the driveway of Claxton Farm and the moment was lost. It had sounded as if he meant to stay and run the farm himself. But that was impossible if he was living in London. Polly put it to the back of her mind. She would ask him later what he meant.

The door was opened by a round, middle-aged woman with rosy cheeks and grey hair drawn up in an old-fashioned bun on top of her head.

'This is my housekeeper, Mrs Moffat,' introduced Jake, as they stepped inside.

Polly shook hands with her as Jake added warmly, 'I couldn't manage without her.'

Mrs Moffat chuckled as she took their rain-sodden coats. 'Don't be deceived by his modesty. Half the time he won't let me cook, but likes to whip up his own strange concoctions.'

Polly looked at Jake, trying to imagine him in the kitchen playing at chef. He gave her a wry grin.

'Now all my secrets will be out once you get chatting to Mrs Moffat.'

Mrs Moffat lifted Laura and gave her a cuddle. 'I think this little lady could definitely do with a bath.'

Laura settled quite happily in her arms. 'I love baths. Can I play with your plastic duck?'

'Let's go upstairs and see if we have such a thing.' The housekeeper and the little girl disappeared up the old staircase, still conversing.

Polly looked around. What a difference there was in the farmhouse. The hall was brightly lit, the walls had been painted, the wood polished and everywhere the scent of beeswax, fresh flowers and the tang of wood smoke coming from a fire in the living room. She could hear it crackle. It might be late spring but on a chill, damp day like this, there was surely nothing better than a roaring fire.

Jake was watching for her reaction. Polly felt touched that he cared what she thought.

She nodded. 'It's wonderful. You've kept Mr Flanagan's photographs too. How lovely to see them cleaned up and on display. They show such a fascinating history of this place.'

'The Australian Mr Flanagan didn't want them, said I could keep or ditch whatever was in the farm. It would have been a crime to discard these.'

He led Polly through to the living room. There was a huge fire burning in the stone fireplace and a brass bucket was stacked with cherry logs ready to fuel it. A comfortable sofa took pride of place in the room with a profusion of colourful cushions scattered around. Polly went to the window and looked out. In old Mr Flanagan's day there had been a kitchen garden beside the house in which he had grown a few vegetables, mainly potatoes and carrots which could look after themselves. Now, Polly could see that the area had been weeded and the earth tilled, ready for new crops. Beyond the low hedge separating the farm garden from the fields, she could see the lambs in an enclosure.

'You've done a lot of work to the place,' she said warmly.

'Not by myself. I have an army of helpers who have shaped the place up in a very short time.'

There were more photographs and sketches framed on the walls. These were not of people but of modern buildings. Polly could see smart blocks of apartments, a conference centre, an unusual building made almost entirely of dark glass, and others. Jake followed her eye.

'These are some of my favourite projects that came to fruition.'

'They look very innovative. No housing estates, then? They all look like city centre developments.'

In other words, completely different to the depressing housing estate that was shortly to destroy Monmeir Loch, thought Polly.

Jake looked surprised. 'Of course they are city centre. Didn't Neil tell you? That's what I do.'

He pointed at an image of a slender tower which incorporated blue ceramic designs, matching tiles on older neighbouring buildings.

'We built this on land where an unsafe Victorian block had stood. It looks great on the outside and in keeping with the historic landscape of housing around it, but that's nothing to how good it is inside. The apartments sold before we'd even finished building it!'

There was an edge of pride in his voice and a real enthusiasm.

Polly said slowly, 'You love it, don't

you? It's art to you.'

'That's it,' Jake agreed, pleased she had caught his point. 'I love giving people beautiful places to work and play and live. It's very, very satisfying.'

'So what on earth are you doing with the Monmeir Loch development?'

Jake sighed. 'I'm doing Uncle Raymond a favour. He had a mild heart attack shortly after the project started, but insisted on keeping going. I was worried he would have another attack if he didn't slow down. So I offered to manage it for him.'

A sense of relief washed over Polly. Suddenly she realised that Jake Grayling wasn't the hard-nosed property developer that she had taken him for, and the knowledge lightened her heart. Maybe they weren't planets apart after all. Maybe there was still room for a meeting of minds and a compromise that suited them both.

'Do you see any value in it?' she asked, still talking about Raymond Rathbone's proposals.

'People need houses to live in that don't cost a fortune.'

'Could you be persuaded to look at an idea of mine, which would give your Uncle Raymond his housing but might actually save the Loch as well?'

Jake had the grace to look embarrassed. 'Polly, I owe you an apology. That day in London when I said I would have the whole thing drained . . .'

'You were angry with me,' Polly said. 'You don't need to explain why, but whatever it was, can you see fit to change your mind?'

'Shoot,' said Jake, and they sat on the sofa amidst the pillows, warming their feet at the fire. Polly's skin was tingling at his nearness. His leg was leaning against hers and she felt a heat which was most definitely not from the fire at his touch. Hesitantly he took her hand in his.

'Jake,' she whispered and, reaching up, kissed him passionately. He returned her kiss, stroking her hair and and murmuring her name.

The sound of footfalls in the hallway made them spring apart. Mrs Moffat arrived with a pot of steaming coffee and a plate of home-made biscuits. Laura had been found a jigsaw, and proceeded to spread out the pieces in front of the fire with great concentration, her hair still damp and wavy from her bath.

Polly had rescued her composure. Jake's dark blue eyes watched her.

'Tell me your idea,' he said, his voice gravelly.

'An eco-village,' said Polly, her eyes flashing. It was her turn now to show enthusiasm for her subject.

'What exactly is that?'

'Imagine this — every house that is built on the site is insulated to reduce heating costs, has solar panels to capture the sun's energy for electricity, is given composting bins to reduce waste. It's a great advertisement for Rathbone's because it would help in the fight against climate change, but also people will be begging to live there because they will reap the benefits of low energy usage.'

'How does that help the wildlife?'

Polly shifted in her seat and glanced at him. 'To be honest, it doesn't. I want to make a bargain with you.'

'Okay. Let's hear it.'

Jake was amused. He could already visualise Raymond Rathbone giving in to Polly's impassioned arguments. She was all aflame like the fire, her hair catching burnished colour from its light, her cheeks flushed and her green eyes vivid. She was beautiful to him, but it was more than that. Her personality was just as attractive as her looks. Jake could drown in her if he let himself. He forced himself to concentrate on what she was saying.

'In return for my great idea and the positive publicity you will get, not to mention the people lining up to live in your carbon-neutral eco-village, you build fewer houses and leave a large area of wild land round the loch as well as Monmeir Loch itself. That way, you can count the natural areas as a contribution to biodiversity, which as you know is a popular part of combating climate change these days too.'

There was a long pause while Jake stared into the flames, his brow furrowed. Polly hardly dared to breathe in case she disturbed him. She crossed her fingers and waited.

Eventually he spoke. 'I think it could work. Let me talk to my team tomorrow. We'll draw up some sketches, get some figures down on paper.'

'Thank you!' Polly could have hugged him.

At that moment Laura gave a huge, loud yawn. They both laughed.

'Time for me to get my niece home, I think.'

'What about the lambs?' protested Laura, as Polly took her by the hand. 'You promised.'

'We'll go and see them now. Once you've got your wellies and coat on,' Jake agreed solemnly. 'A promise mustn't be broken.'

Polly followed them from the room. *I could be a mother*, she thought unexpectedly, *if the father was like Jake*. She drove the thought from her mind. But a tendril of it stayed with her as she briskly buttoned her coat to go and see the baby lambs. *If the father was Jake*. They watched Laura as she walked round the enclosure talking to each lamb in turn.

Jake said, 'Polly, about us . . . '

She cut in quickly. 'Let's forget it ever happened. It was the heat of the moment, wasn't it?' She was gabbling now, wishing herself elsewhere.

'There was heat in the moment, yes. But I can't forget that it happened. If you are honest, can you?' He tilted her head up so she had to meet his dark blue gaze.

Polly flushed. 'No,' she whispered. She stood on tiptoes and wrapped her arms around him. Jake grinned, lifted her off her feet and spun her around. She shrieked and Laura shrieked happily too to keep her company.

They drove in contented silence back to Polly's parents' house. Jake lifted Laura down from the Land Rover.

'Let me take you out tomorrow,' suggested Polly impetuously. 'I want to show you something.'

'Mmm, sounds mysterious,' he said, with a playful quirk of his brow. 'An offer I could not refuse.'

'Tomorrow morning, then. Please pick me up here. I'll be waiting.'

She could hardly bear to let him go. *I love him, I love him*, she sang inwardly. She and Laura watched the Land Rover disappear round the corner of the road, then they made their way inside.

8

Lou had arranged to meet Ian at a coffee house in a coastal town outside Glasgow. It was neutral territory and a place where they were very unlikely to bump into any of their friends or relatives. As she walked nervously to join her husband, Lou listened to the keening of the seagulls above. They circled and glided, screaming into the wind. It sounded sad, and in keeping with her heart. Could she and Ian really resolve their differences over a cup of coffee?

She saw him through the window of the cafe. He was drumming his fingers on the table as if playing an imaginary piano. Chopin at his most savage. The Grand Waltz, perhaps. So Ian was just as nervous as she was. Somehow that made Lou calmer. She had half thought he had made up his mind to leave her and Laura, and this was to be goodbye.

She opened the door. Ian looked up and smiled. It was strained. He stood awkwardly until she had settled into the chair opposite.

'What would you like? The capuccino here is excellent, so is their house expresso. I've been here a few times because of work and . . . '

Lou stopped him by placing her hand over his. 'Ian, tell me. I have to know. Are you leaving me for good?'

He drew in a sharp breath and seemed to slump before her eyes, in shock. 'No! No, Lou.'

'What then? You haven't been home for days. What else am I to think?'

He stroked her hand, then tightened his grasp on it. He looked at her until she raised her head to look at him.

'I haven't been honest with you, Lou. I'm so sorry. I have wanted to tell you for a long time.'

This was it. He was having an affair. He had been unfaithful to her. Lou went pale. 'There's someone else, isn't there?'

He shook his head. The waitress came to take their order. Lou spoke automatically. Afterwards she wasn't sure what she had asked for. They waited until the woman had gone again before speaking.

'Lou, I've behaved badly towards you and Laura. I feel guilty even thinking about it. But Laura's tantrums, the yelling and the chaos in the house have all been the last straws for the camel.'

The English teacher part of Lou wanted to correct his idiom but she listened in silence, still unsure where this was leading.

'The truth is, I'm very unhappy at work. I hate my job. I've wanted to leave it for so long but I'm the breadwinner so I can't. I feel physically sick every morning getting the train and pushing open those office doors.'

'Why didn't you tell me?' Lou was at once relieved that he wasn't having an affair, and angry that he had bottled everything up and not confided in her at all.

'How could I? You deserve time at home with Laura. It's important that you are there when she is small and needs you. We need the money, so I need to work. It's that simple.'

Lou sipped her coffee to give herself time to think. Her hands were shaky on the cup. What a bombshell he had dropped. Why had she not noticed anything amiss? Why had it taken a bitter argument and Ian disappearing to live elsewhere for her to pick up on his unhappiness?

'You are not the only one to blame,' she said slowly, putting her cup down carefully onto the saucer. 'I should have seen what you were going through. I've been so focused on Laura that I've neglected you.'

Ian looked at her for a long moment, his expression full of tenderness.

'I love you, Lou. I always have and I always will. I don't blame you. I just don't know where we go from here.'

'Well, I do. Laura has a free place waiting for her at nursery. I was going to speak to you about it but there was never an opportunity. I think it would do her good to mix with other children. Actually, I need a break too. I want to go back to teaching part-time. If I did that, could you cut your hours? Or is it time for you to branch out on your own, set up your own business the way you always dreamed?'

It was a long speech. It poured out of her and Lou realised she had wanted to say it to Ian quite some time ago. She had been thinking about it. Yes, it was scary to think of managing on less money until Ian's business established but if she worked mornings she could bring in enough for them to get by. Most importantly, they would be a team, and together they would make it work.

'I didn't realise you wanted a break from being at home.'

'We're both guilty of not noticing each other,' answered Lou honestly.

'How will Laura be around other kids? She's acting so badly, would the nursery take her?'

Lou rubbed her forehead. 'I don't know what's got into her. We can only try and see how she gets on. Maybe she needs a break from us too.'

They paid at the till and walked hand in hand along the promenade, the wind whipping their hair and flushing their faces.

'Come home, Ian,' Lou said quietly as they watched the white sails of the dinghies racing in the estuary.

Ian hugged her tightly. 'Of course. Let's go and get my stuff right now.'

'The house is still messy and Laura is still out of sorts,' she reminded him, glancing up.

'I don't care. The thought of handing in my notice this week makes everything feel fantastic. Thank you, Lou.' He bent and kissed her.

Lou wrapped her arms around her husband and vowed never to let him go again.

★　★　★

Croombs Wood was like a slice of paradise on a sunny day. The season was sliding lazily from late spring to summer and the flowers were blossoming, bees humming and birds nesting in timeless cycles of nature. Polly breathed in the fresh, warm air and felt truly happy.

Jake had picked her up promptly that morning and she had given him instructions to find the woods. He looked at her quizzically. 'Much as I enjoy a mystery tour, any particular reason for the blindfold?'

'As you are driving, I hope very much you don't have a blindfold,' Polly retorted, laughing. 'I don't want to tell you about the place we are going because I want you to feel its impact for yourself.'

And here they were. Polly looked at Jake for his reaction. He was gazing around with a smile. So far, so good.

'Mum has packed enough picnic food for about ten people,' said Polly, rummaging in the boot. She pulled out a wicker hamper and groaned at the weight of it. Jake took it from her as if it was nothing.

'If we follow this trail through the woods, we will find Gallows Glade where we can eat our banquet.'

'Gallows Glade? Sounds charming.'

'It's not as grim as it sounds. You'll see.'

Polly led them along the trail between tall trees of oak and ash and maple and with occasional majestic Scots pine. The ground was a soft bed of leaf and pine needles with nodding bluebells, white stars of wood anemone and stitchwort and pink blankets of purslane and herb robert. Speckled butterflies flitted from sunpatch to sunpatch in the dappled light and everywhere there was the scent of warmed earth, green plants and per-fumed petals.

'Aromatherapy laid on,' Jake com-mented as a waft of honeysuckle reached them.

'Very relaxing,' agreed Polly. 'You

know there is lots of research now, which shows that people who walk in natural surroundings have better physical and mental health than people who don't.'

'Why is that?' Jake sounded intrigued.

'No-one knows. It's something intangible, but has a real effect. People need nature. We don't always appreciate it or value it, but human beings are dependent on it for health and well-being.'

'I'm beginning to see why we are visiting Croombs Wood,' Jake said drily. 'It's not just a picnic on a holiday Monday, is it, Polly?'

'Don't be angry,' she said quickly, 'I want you to see what I see when I walk in Croombs Wood or by Monmeir Loch or a thousand other such places. Please let me show you.'

Jake looked at her earnest face with its intense green eyes and that so-touchable hair. He didn't care why Polly had brought him here. It was enough to drink in the sight of her and to listen to her voice and to smell her familiar violet fragrance.

'Lead me to the Gallows,' he said in a dreadful, Gothic tone.

'So it shall be. But on the way to your ghastly end, let me try to explain why all this is so important.'

Jake's only answer was to throw some pine needles at her.

Polly grabbed a clump of grass and tried to stick it down his collar. Jake dropped the hamper and ran after her. Polly raced like mad, almost hysterical with laughter. Jake was gaining on her. With a final spurt of energy she burst into Gallows Glade and was felled by a long rugby tackle. Polly yelled and sat up, still giggling. Jake was breathing heavily, still wearing a grass necklace and grinning.

'All those years of private school sport finally paid off.'

'You win,' agreed Polly, 'But where's the picnic?'

'For you, fair lady, I will retrieve it before I meet my doom. Where is the gallows tree, by the way?'

'No idea, it's been a picnic spot for years. Come on, I'll help you get the hamper.'

They retraced their steps and took a handle each of the discarded picnic box. They settled on a wooden table and chairs in the glade and Polly unpacked the various plastic bags and foil parcels.

The glade was a large, open, grassy space ringed by the woods. There were several picnic tables and benches and scattered metal blocks for barbecues. Little paths radiated out from the glade and meandered amongst the trees enticingly. Some were man-made but others were formed by deer, badgers and foxes. Polly pointed them out to Jake and described the night life in Croombs Wood as nocturnal animals became active and took over from their daytime cousins.

'There are bats, too. See the bat boxes up there.' Polly pointed at small wooden boxes high up on the trees, which had been installed by her mother, Isla and Mel as part of the Croombs Wood friendship group — people who used the woods and felt strongly that the community should look after it.

'Would those boxes be good in the eco-village?' asked Jake, selecting another of Mrs Baker's angel cakes.

Polly looked at him warmly. 'Yes, very much. So you have given my idea more thought?'

'I like it in principle. I'm not sure how well it will translate in practice. As I said, I need to talk to my team back in the office.'

'Why were you so angry with me during the meeting with Rathbone?' Polly asked impulsively.

Jake put down the angel cake slowly. He crumbled a piece of it onto the grass, to the delight of a hungry robin. Then he looked straight at Polly.

'It was unforgivable. I shouldn't have let my emotions get in the way of my work. But you unsettled me, Polly.'

'Unsettled?'

'You are very attractive. I was annoyed at myself for noticing that. I took it out on you by demanding we drain the loch.'

'You think I'm attractive?' Polly zoned in on this delightful confession, Monmeir Loch for once ignored. Her face lit up and her heart sang its song.

'You are pretty, vivacious and funny,' Jake said, his voice deep, his blue eyes dark as he looked at her, 'and you catch me off guard every time we talk. I never know what to expect.'

'Is that a good thing?' murmured Polly, reaching for him.

'Very,' came the answer some time later after many passionate kisses.

'I love you,' she whispered into his chest as he hugged her close. But the words were smothered by his shirt. He'd not mentioned love, but he liked her and was attracted to her and that was a start.

There was a cheery call and three small children ran into the clearing from the opposite side of the glade, closely followed by a small terrier and two women. Jake and Polly moved a little apart, and Polly opened the flask of coffee and poured two cups. They watched the family as they set up camp on the far side of Gallows Glade. The older woman spread out a patterned rug and proceeded to lay out food. The younger woman, obviously the mother, kicked a ball about with the children and encouraged their efforts with much calling and applauding of goals. The terrier barked and wagged its tail and generally caused havoc by scampering between legs and jumping up at its family.

As Polly and Jake enjoyed watching this entertaining tableau a fox suddenly appeared at the woods' edge. He was handsome, a rich, glossy red colour with fine plumed tail. The mother called softly to the children and they stopped their play to see it. The oldest child grabbed the dog and hunkered with it to keep it quiet. The fox wasn't bothered about the people. He sniffed the air and trotted, dog-like, along the glade perimeter, until he slipped silently back into the darkness of the trees.

There was delighted chatter from the family as they ran over to the grandmother on the rug for their picnic.

Jake turned to Polly and they smiled at one another.

'That was magical,' Jake said. 'I'm beginning to understand what you mean about people and nature. Just the look on those kids' faces when they saw the fox — it was a treat.'

She took his hands. 'Help me then, Jake. You have the power to make a difference to the places where people live. Imagine having a house in a setting which included glades and hedgerows and the possibility of seeing foxes and countless other wild creatures every day to lift the soul.'

Jake was lost in thought as they packed up the hamper and wandered back to the Land Rover. Polly kept quiet, letting him mull it all over. She was content to listen to the birdsong and see the dragonflies hunting next to the Croombs Burn.

When they were driving away, she told him.

'Croombs Wood is going to be destroyed to make way for a trunk road.'

Jake could hear the pain in her voice. He caressed her cheek, stroked her hair and kissed her gently. There was nothing to say.

* * *

Jake woke the next morning and knew what he had to do. He phoned the airport, booked his flight to London, showered and dressed quickly. Over a brief breakfast of scrambled eggs on toast he phoned Nina, arranging to meet her at a restaurant near to her Kensington apartment early that afternoon. He also phoned Shanna. Once he had made these simple arrangements, Jake began to feel better and brighter.

He was not looking forward to his meetings with Nina or his mother, and dreaded what he had to tell them, but at least he had put his plans in motion and it had begun.

As the aeroplane flew down the coast, he gazed out unseeingly at pale beaches, white trims of waves where the sea crashed against the rugged land and wisps and strands of cotton clouds decorating the sky on an unexpectedly beautiful day. His mind was full of thoughts of Polly and Nina. The conflict that had been raging inside him since he kissed Polly Baker had to be resolved. Although duty to his mother and to the Grayling name had always been his priority, for the first time in his life Jake realised that he had to put his own feelings and desires to the fore.

Shanna fully expected him to marry Nina; she would make a beautiful addition to the public lives they lived, but Jake was no longer sure of himself, his lifestyle or anything else. The firm rock beneath him had shifted with warm kisses from a scatterbrained redhead. Jake grimaced as the plane arrived at Heathrow. A final duty had to be dealt with, and it would be an unpleasant one.

Nina was sitting composedly against a backdrop of charcoal velvet sofa which showed off her lemon hair and grey eyes to perfection. The restaurant was busy but the maitre d' had ushered her to a quiet corner and attended personally to her drinks order. Nina was that kind of woman, who expected and received men's homage as her due. But with Jake she had felt some effort had always been required to keep him hooked.

'Darling,' she breathed now with a cupid smile.

'Nina.' Jake nodded, kissing her chastely on the cheek, avoiding her lips. 'Thanks for seeing me at short notice.'

She made a little moue of her mouth. 'Don't be silly, darling, I was dying to see you. Besides, the chocolate advert is finished and I'm waiting for my agent to call. There's so little work about just now.'

Jake gently removed her hand from where it lay on his. 'I'll come straight to the point, Nina. I know my mother has encouraged you to anticipate us getting back together but I have to be blunt. It's never going to happen.'

He looked her in the eye firmly as he spoke, steeling himself her reaction and her tears. Nina flushed and for a moment he thought she would slap him as she raised her hand in a flash but as quickly dropped it to her lap. Her brittle smile did not reach her eyes as she said coolly, 'Why, have you found someone else? Don't tell me it's your little red-headed secretary. Goodness, you move fast, in keeping with your playboy reputation!'

Jake winced. His reputation for working hard and playing hard had been fed to the media by his mother as a ploy to generate business and publicity. But it certainly worked. There were many businessmen, entrepreneurs and companies who thought it no bad thing for a man to have a string of beautiful women beside him and to be in the limelight as a result. Business did well out of constant media coverage of parties, receptions, charity engagements and so on. The reality of it was rather different, as Jake knew. The girls were usually models desperate for fame, only too happy to accompany him to a dinner and ball knowing quite well they would leave alone in a chauffeur-driven limousine at Jake's expense. There had been very few love affairs along the way; he did not regret that.

'I don't want to hurt you, Nina,' he replied, ignoring her barbs, 'but I don't love you and I cannot see a future for us. I'm sorry.'

'Love!' she sneered, two ugly blotches of red appearing on her cheeks. 'Who's talking about love? We have a business agreement. You need a beautiful wife on your arm and I need a decent lifestyle. I don't love you, Jacob Grayling, but I do need you. And you need me.'

Jake was speechless. Nina's soft, sophisticated veneer had vanished and in place of her cool, ice beauty there was an ugliness that stunned him. What a fool he had been. He'd always known she did not love him, but he had thought they at least liked each other. He started to rise but she grabbed his arm.

'Have your fun with the Baker girl if you like, but don't run out on your mother's deal. It would be foolish.'

'Foolish indeed,' repeated a sharp voice behind them. Jake swung round to see Shanna Grayling. She slipped into the seat beside him, her jaw tight and eyes like flint. 'Thank you for inviting me to lunch Jacob,' she said calmly, picking up a menu and scanning it briskly.

A waiter appeared and she ordered. 'Lemon sole and a green salad for each of us. Oh, and bottled spring water.' The man bowed and glided off.

'Duty, Jacob, remember? You have a duty to me as your mother and a duty to the family and the media empire. Don't throw it all away on a whim.'

A whim. Jake thought of Polly, standing in the breeze on top of the hill not far from Claxton Farm, her red curls wild and free, face alive with her fierce determination and passion for the outdoors. Her strong sense of right and wrong when it came to Monmeir Loch. With a jolt, he knew with certainty that he had fallen in love with her. She was not 'his type', they were leading very different lives, but none of that mattered. She was not a whim. His heart sang. Suddenly he was desperate to get back to Scotland to tell her. But Shanna Grayling was still speaking, gently now as if to a cornered animal that may bolt.

'Let us not be hasty. Nina is right. It is a comfortable arrangement. Nina will make you a perfect wife. Many of the best business deals are made over dinner and a married man with an attractive, competent wife is favourably looked upon. You are already a wealthy man, Jacob, but that's nothing compared to what we can achieve together!'

'Money isn't everything, Shanna,' he replied bitterly. 'As for duty, I have been a dutiful son to you since I was five years old. I have toed the party line. Now I want to do what is right for me. I will give up my shares in the company to you. In return, all I ask is that you drop the glare of publicity and PR. I'm going to buy Claxton Farm and live there.'

'With this Polly person?'

'Perhaps, in time. If she'll have me.'

'Very well.' Shanna nodded slowly, gesturing to Nina who would have spoken. 'I accept your offer of shares and in return for getting the media off your back, I ask only one thing.'

Jake quirked an eyebrow. This was too easy. His mother usually fought like steel.

Shanna went on, 'Promise me you won't carry out your plan or tell Polly until after the Mayor's charity ball. I have a lot of deals coming to fruition then and it would help if you and Nina went together and harmoniously to avoid any adverse gossip until these are clinched.'

Jake nodded his agreement and glanced at Nina to see her reaction. Nina was looking unusually pensive and managed another small artificial smile. *No point wasting emotion on him now*, it seemed to say. *Now that the gloves are off.*

'I agree with Shanna. And maybe by then you'll have come to your senses.' She rose in a waft of expensive vanilla scent and kissed him lightly before leaving the restaurant. Jake stayed with Shanna to eat.

'Is it serious, with this young woman?'

'I love her,' he said simply.

'Does she love you?'

'I don't know, to be absolutely honest. But I'm prepared to take that risk.'

Shanna spoke steadily now as if afraid he would interrupt. 'I have only

146

ever had your best interests at heart, Jacob. You were very young when your father died. And so was I. It wasn't easy being left along with a small child to raise. I made a decision to work hard at my career so that you would have everything you needed for a decent start in life. Money is security. That is what I could give you.'

She stopped to dab her mouth with the napkin. Jake said nothing, did not want to divert her in any way. This was the first time she had opened up like this and he wanted to hear it. All of it.

She continued, still with little inflection, as if reining in her emotions.

'I loved your father. But it wasn't enough. He was a dreamer. He meandered through life, expecting things to turn up for the best. None of his schemes came to fruition. We were struggling financially when he died. He left nothing to provide for us. That was when I knew that I had to use my brains and my family connections to build a life for you.'

'I didn't know,' said Jake, appalled. 'You let me believe Dad was a hero, all these years.'

'He was a hero. To you. Why would I spoil your memories? He was a charming, loving father and husband. In the end, it was up to me to be the practical one. I was never good at being demonstrative. I've not been a good mother in that sense. But you have never wanted for anything material.'

Jake was too astonished to speak. He looked at Shanna as if really seeing her for the first time. He saw in her face the young woman she had been, left abandoned with a five-year-old son and no means of support.

'The game plan, Jacob, is about care and protection. Of you. I want you to be happy and successful.'

'But it's not my game plan, Shanna. It's yours. I can't play it any more.'

He was preparing to leave when Shanna put her hand on his arm. He turned. She cleared her throat, played with the napkin before speaking.

'I am proud of you, Jake. Very proud indeed of how you have turned out. I hope very much to be invited to Claxton Farm to visit you and Polly some day soon.'

Her face had softened and her eyes glistened. Jake hugged his mother, feeling her bones angular and unused to yielding to an embrace. He held on until he felt her hug him back. Then, afraid he would cry too, he hurried from the restaurant to catch his plane home.

In the air, the scheduled flight surprisingly on time, and longing for Polly and the peace of Claxton, he mused on what had happened.

It would be torture seeing Polly and yet being unable to tell her of his feelings, but if it would help Shanna then it was only fair. It was barely a week until the Mayor's Ball and in the meantime he could hole up at Claxton farm in its now familiar, wonderful atmosphere of home.

9

Polly had been invited round to Lou's house. Her sister had phoned excitedly to explain that Ian had come home, and to tell Polly how it had come about. Polly went round after work, hoping that Laura would not be too noisy. She had a thumping headache from a hectic day, so busy that there had not been time even for lunch.

Lou opened the door after one ring of the doorbell. She looked much better than when Polly had last seen her. Lou's face was a healthy colour and the bags under her eyes had vanished. There was a sparkle to her and she grabbed her sister and pulled her inside.

'Ian's not here. He's out talking to our accountant to draw up his business plan. He's so excited, and so am I.'

As she chatted, Lou led the way into

the living room. It was spotless. There was a big box of toys but it was stacked neatly to one side of the room. The sofa was clean, the cushions were all in place and the carpet had clearly been vacuumed that day. The house smelt of beeswax and lavender and fresh flowers. There was a gigantic bouquet in a crystal vase on the coffee table, tied with an elaborate bow. Polly guessed they were from Ian even before she saw the little note attached. Just a love heart and his initial.

The escritoire, which was Polly's favourite piece of furniture in her sister's house, was piled with teacher's manuals and lesson ideas.

Polly nodded towards it. 'Getting ready for the new term?'

'Yes, I've got plenty of time before school starts in August, but I want to get back into practice. I've managed to get a place three mornings a week in the school up the road. It's perfect. I can take Laura to nursery before nine and pick her up at lunch time.'

'Where is my little niece? Is she out? It's so quiet.'

'She's upstairs, drawing.'

'What's happened? She never usually has the concentration for that.'

Lou went to the kitchen and returned with an empty juice bottle. On it were cartoon pictures of raspberries and blackberries. She waggled it at Polly who frowned, puzzled.

'Okay, I give in. What's with the plastic bottle?'

'Well, you know it's Laura's favourite diluting juice. She drinks it all the time. But I ran out of it a few days ago and was too tired and out of sorts to get more in. Once she'd rampaged about it, she forgot to ask for it. After a couple of days, I noticed a real change in her. She wasn't so angry, she was calmer and she could sit for longer drawing, modelling clay or whatever.'

'You think the juice was responsible for her moods?' Polly asked incredulously.

'I'm absolutely convinced of it. I read

about it on the internet. Some children can't tolerate additives and food colourings. It makes them antsy. They can't concentrate, they have mood swings, the lot, just as she had!'

'That's fantastic, Lou. I'm glad everything is back to normal.'

Lou pulled her down onto the sofa. 'So tell me about Jake and about the Mayor's Ball. What will you wear? Will Jake give you a corsage? Or is that old-fashioned? I read it in a romance.'

Polly sighed. 'Mum's been at it again, hasn't she? There's never any news for me to tell you. The only thing I can add is that Jake and I are not going together to the Ball.'

'Why ever not?'

'His mother asked him to escort Nina instead. They do make a stunning couple and it's all to help with some media coverage she needs.'

'And you believed her?'

'No. But I do believe Jake. He and Nina are just friends. And if he can help his mother, then of course he should take Nina to the Ball. I'm going with Harriet and Neil and we'll have a fun time, whatever happens.'

Polly said all this firmly so that Lou would not try to persuade her otherwise. She did believe Jake. Of course she did. There was a tiny, traitorous part of her that doubted, but the rest of her was fine with it. The only thing was that she didn't trust Nina or Shanna. They clearly did not want Polly around. Were they demanding that Jake accompany Nina to the Ball for some other reason than publicity? Nina was glamorous and beautiful. Was it expecting too much of Jake not to be seduced by her? She knew that Shanna's game plan involved Nina. Was it time for the game plan to be played out?

What would happen when Jake left the Monmeir project and returned to London? Was it too much to hope that they would still be . . . what? What were they to each other anyway? Polly's mind buzzed with questions. She and Jake seemed to be growing closer, were most definitely attracted to each other and learning about each other more deeply each time they met. But they were not an item. He had never mentioned love. And though she had, only the wind had heard that day at Croombs Wood.

* * *

Polly gazed at her reflection in the tall mirror and grimaced. Was the bodice too revealing? Then the door burst open and Harriet appeared, flushed and excited in shimmering peach satin.

'Oh, you look lovely, Polly,' she exclaimed. 'What a tiny waist, you lucky thing!'

'Is the colour too bold?' asked Polly diffidently. She fingered the shot green silk, feeling its deliciously smooth texture.

'It makes your hair all flames,' laughed Harriet, giving her a hug that threatened to crush Polly's gown before she had even arrived at the reception. Harriet herself, complete with pearl

155

drop earrings, looked elegant and radiant.

'Quite a change from waterproofs and muddy wellies, isn't it?'

'Don't get too used to it,' Polly warned, slipping a tiny gold stud into each ear lobe. 'I don't really think Green Lives should be here at all. It's not our sort of thing.'

'Nonsense,' rebuffed Harriet. 'Neil's delighted to bring us to London, even if it does mean splashing out on this gorgeous hotel. It's great exposure for the consultancy. Why, we might even see our faces in the celebrity magazines tomorrow!'

She gave a mock shriek and pretended to read from an invisible magazine. 'Lady Pauline Baker and Dame Harriet Summers attended the Mayor's Charity all last night.'

Polly leaned over her shoulder and pointed at a pretend page. 'Guests of honour and invited to sit at the Mayor's table for dinner no less,' she joked.

'Chance would be a fine thing,'

snorted Harriet, 'But we'll still have fun wherever we sit. Must dash, I've still to apply a last coat of nail varnish. See you down there!'

Polly carefully touched a dash of shimmering green to her eyelids. She would see Jake tonight. Her heart fluttered. Since his return from London, he had been distant and busy. There had been no opportunity to speak to him further about her plans for the eco-village. Occasionally she had looked up from her work in her office to see him gazing at her from beyond the glass of the main office. He had turned away quickly and she was never sure then if he had been looking at her or simply staring into space. It was hard to believe they had ever spent time together at Claxton Farm so intimately, sharing confidences like old trusted friends, or perhaps with the promise of more.

Was she right to worry about Nina? Polly had felt uneasy, but tried to put it out of her mind. Maybe he was simply busy. She would catch up with him at the Ball.

She had just finished doing her make-up when there was another knock on the door. Neil stood there, his hair for once smoothed down for the occasion, smart in a tuxedo and bow tie.

'Gosh, don't you look distinguished!' teased Polly.

'You clean up well yourself,' came the reply with a cheeky grin.

'What is this, the mutual admiration society?' chipped in Harriet who had arrived behind Neil in the corridor.

He turned to greet her and she gasped.

'I had no idea what a handsome boss I had.' There was a little gleam in her blue eyes that made Polly think of hunter and prey. Well, Neil could take care of himself. She herded them out of the room, tucked a final curl behind her ear and prepared for the ball to begin.

The music rose to greet them as they descended the wide, plushly carpeted staircase. The massive reception hall was warm from so many people gathering there and the chat and laughter rose and fell in waves forming a backdrop to the music of a string quartet. The male guests were uniformly clad in dark dinner jackets, tuxedos, bow ties and shiny shoes. Their female companions, by contrast, were butterflies of emerald, turquoise, lilac and a hundred shades in between. Polly's nose twitched as a swathe of perfumes hit it and she was glad she had not sprayed any on herself but had settled for a dab of essential oil.

Harriet grabbed Neil's arm and dragged him off to admire a painting coincidentally close to a table laden with champagne and canapes. Waiters glided through the throng, offering the same from tiny silver trays. Polly accepted a slim flute of sparkling wine and stood uncertainly for a moment. She knew no one, and hated the thought of mingling and making polite conversation with people she would likely never see again after this evening.

There was a lull in the conversation, one of those strange short-lived silences which happen periodically in crowds. *An angel flying overhead*, Polly's gran had always claimed when it occurred at family gatherings. At the same time the groups in front of her thinned, and she saw him. Jake Grayling. He was turned slightly away, searching for someone in the masses, and she had an opportunity to admire him and feel love squeeze her heart painfully. His tall frame was perfectly suited to the immaculate dinner jacket which outlined his powerful shoulders and tapered waist. He caught sight of her and his eyes brightened. He strode towards her with a smile and Polly realised happily that it was for her he had been scanning the crowd.

'Polly! You look . . . ' He paused and his blue eyes darkened. 'Beautiful.'

Flustered, Polly made a mock curtsey but he pulled her up gently and said, 'I have to speak to you after the ball. It's important.' The urgency of his tone surprised her.

'Okay, I'll meet you in the Gold Room on the opposite side of the foyer afterwards.'

Jake looked as if he would have said more but suddenly Nina was there, linking arms firmly with him and nodding politely at Polly. Polly's joy at her dress and shoes spiralled downwards. Beside Nina she felt fat and frumpy. Nina's dress was a Grecian design of the palest sky blue, delicately clasped over one shoulder with a jewelled brooch, leaving one perfect shoulder bare. Her exquisite shoes had the most impossible slender heels which added to her model height, making her on an eye level with Jake. Polly had to crane her neck up to look at them.

'Darling, it's time to find our table for dinner. I believe the Mayor is about to welcome us all.'

'Excuse us, Polly.' Jake's intense expression sent her a message she could not read as he escorted Nina expertly between people to the top table.

'I must find my own table and rescue Neil from Harriet,' Polly replied lightly and stepped into the moving crowd. *What on earth could Jake have to say that is so important?* she wondered as someone trod on her toes.

She elbowed rather rudely through the last cluster and found Harriet and Neil sitting contentedly at a round table laden with crystal glasses and shining silverware, sharing a last canape. Polly plumped herself down beside them, still musing on Jake's strange behaviour. The only thing she could imagine was that he had had some new ideas for the eco-village. But why look so serious?

Harriet nudged her. The Mayor was beginning his welcome speech. It went on for a very long time, full of good wishes and thanks to the guests, the various benefactors and fundraisers and the wonderful projects that were helping investment in the city. At last he finished, to loud applause, and the soup course began to arrive, table by table.

162

Polly looked around at the lavish decorations, the glitter of crystal, the expensive silks and drop diamonds. It would be hard to calculate the wealth crammed in to this one large room. It was an alien environment for her, far from her beloved marshes and wide open skies. Suddenly it was all too much for her.

'Why are we here, Neil?' Polly burst out.

Neil was so startled, he spilt his consommé. They both watched the yellow liquid being absorbed into the fine white linen tablecloth.

'You know why, Polly. It's a chance for Green Lives to promote itself, get new clients. What's the matter with you?' Neil was exasperated. Now was not the time for one of Polly's outbursts of environmental conscience.

'This event is all about investment. Business. Money. Not about green issues. We are an environmental company; why are we down here?'

'As you know fine well, we currently

work for a London client. Okay, I admit they are not an environmentally-friendly client but that is where you come in. You are supposed to use your powers of persuasion to get them to think green.'

'And I have! Or is an eco-village not green enough? For goodness' sake, Neil, what more can I do?'

'What eco-village? What are you talking about?'

'Did Jake not tell you?'

Polly was bewildered. She hadn't seen the new landscape design plans herself yet but that was because she had hidden away in her office, frantically overloaded with reports and files. Surely he had told Neil of the plan overhaul; its complete revision?

The room felt hot and stuffy, cloying with smells of roast pork, floral scents and sweat. Polly staggered to her feet, her face white.

'I need some air,' she mumbled to a concerned Harriet, shaking her head when Harriet offered to come with her.

Neil sat, his hair returned to its spiky state as he ran tense fingers through it. Polly left Harriet looking reproachfully at him and made her way carefully to the foyer, skirting the dining tables with guests now tucking into pork leg, roast potatoes and apple sauce with a spaghetti of seasonal vegetables.

The ladies' powder room lay discreetly down a short corridor to the left of the hotel entrance. It was the size of Polly's flat. Tranquil music played quietly in the background. Large bouquets of pink roses and baby's breath lined the sinks with their gold taps and pristine china bowls. There were fluffy cream towels, pretty boxes of facial tissues and fresh face flannels rolled neatly with silk bows. Polly saw herself reflected into many diminishing Pollys in the magnificent mirrors adorning the walls. Each little Polly looked pale and sick and anxious.

She splashed cold water on to her face and rubbed her cheeks to add some colour. Behind her the door opened and Nina entered the powder room.

'Polly, you look terrible,' she said in sympathetic, honeyed tones, coming to stand beside her at the sinks. 'I saw you leaving the dinner and wondered if you needed some help?'

Nina was the last person Polly wanted help from. Had Nina really been so concerned for her that she had followed her here? She hesitated. It was tempting to tell someone how she felt. It was impossible to confide in her mother or in Lou, who had had enough problems of her own recently. Harriet, though a dear friend, was too much of a gossip to be able to keep any secrets, and would trickle it to Neil who would disapprove and might even take her off the project. But Nina?

Impossible to confess that she, Polly, had fallen deeply, so very deeply, in love with her boss. And that her belief in him had been shaken by Neil's denial of the eco-village plans. Add her suspicions about Shanna setting up Nina as the perfect escort for her son and no, she could not talk to anyone about it all.

Nina touched up her already immaculate make-up in the mirror.

'I know what will cheer you up,' she said. 'The design layouts for the Monmeir Loch development are on display in the Gold Room. It will be cooler there. That will give you a chance to recover before returning for dessert.'

'It is awfully hot,' murmured Polly, allowing herself to be drawn, not unwillingly, out of the powder room and along the corridor to the ornately decorated Gold Room.

The displays of development projects, from all the companies invited to the reception, stood looking incongruously modern against the decor of gilt and cherubs. The air was thankfully cool and Polly sighed gratefully. The room was empty and silent but for the click of their heels as Nina guided her through the forest of boards until they were facing

'Rathbone Development Company' in bold lettering atop five panels of text, sketches and diagrams.

'Jake is very proud of the design,' Nina said smoothly. 'In fact he was boasting to me that he had managed to squeeze in a whole segment of extra housing over the east edge of the loch. That will boost his profit margins considerably.'

She laughed prettily, her grey eyes flashing at Polly to see her reaction. Polly's stomach clenched. Her fingers were icy-cold as she stepped forward to stare at the centre design. It blurred in front of her as she connected images, conscious of Nina watching her. The design showed sketches of Monmeir Loch. The first showed the loch in its present state; the gentle curving outline of its edges, the marshes and islands and the countryside around it. The second sketch was dotted with tiny squares representing houses. And the shape of Monmeir Loch had changed dramatically. The loch had been cut in half by a large rectangular building. This must be what Nina was alluding to. Jake had not only revoked her (and his, she had thought) vision for the exemplary eco-village, he had gone the other way entirely and built houses all over the wetlands just like a hard-nosed property developer would do.

Now she knew why Jake had been so distant this last week. Why he had made himself scarce every time she had tried to speak to him or to make eye contact. It also explained his odd behaviour this evening and his desire to meet her here in the Gold Room. He still had some vestige of honour, she presumed, to want to confess to her his complete turnaround. It was a renunciation of her and all she stood for. Why had she ever thought well of him? She had trusted him. And she had been wrong.

Polly felt sick to her stomach. The whole loch area was destroyed. All the wonderful wildlife and grandeur of nature ripped up and replaced with concrete and brick. And for what? To line Jake's pockets and those of his Uncle Raymond. Well, he had shown his true colours at last. His idea of an ideal development was a thousand miles removed from hers and she realised now that they could never meet in the middle. Compromise had proved to be impossible.

Nina was talking. Polly struggled to zone in to what she was saying.

'Stick around for the end of the evening. There's going to be a surprise announcement.'

'I don't feel very well. I think I may leave early.'

'But if you do that you will miss Jake's speech.'

'Jake's giving a speech? Of thanks to the mayor?'

Nina laughed her tinkling laugh. 'Better than that by far. It's the announcement of our engagement to be married.'

Afterwards, Polly was glad that she had not crumpled or wept hot tears as she desperately wished to do. She managed to whisper her congratulations through numb lips before slipping from the Gold Room and running up the grand staircase until she reached the sanctuary of her room.

It was silly to feel so devastated. She was an idiot! Jake had never been hers. He had never promised her any such thing. It had always been clear that he and Nina were close friends. But Polly couldn't forget the time that they had spent together as friends at Claxton Farm, nor the satisfaction they had both seemed to get from climbing the hill behind her parents' house and seeing the tiny pipit's nest. They were small events in themselves, but she had enjoyed his company, had warmed to him as he opened up to her and she could not help falling in love with him. Nor could she forget the searing pleasure of his kisses.

Perhaps in time I will be able to fall out of love with him, she thought grimly, pulling her green silk dress off none too gently as if it was the enemy.

She took her earrings out and flung them on the bed, then flung herself after them and sobbed and sobbed into the pillows. When she was wrung dry, Polly sat up, wiped her damp face with her hand and dragged her suitcase from under the bed. It was time to go home.

10

Polly leaned her face against the cold glass of the bus window and watched the blur of coloured lights against the darkness as London flew past. She had briefly considered flying home and billing Jacob Grayling for it but commonsense had prevailed and here she was on the overnight bus from London Victoria to Glasgow Buchanan Street. The bus was packed; it was surprising how many people were up in the middle of the night. Victoria bus station had been bustling, noisy, smelly and a relief after the debacle of the Mayor's Ball. Polly had got the last available ticket and now was wedged in to the window seat by a very large lady who sat sucking peppermints and crocheting an alarmingly long scarf.

Polly watched the old fingers flick

rhythmically over the wool. It was hypnotic and helped to blank her mind. She felt wrung out. Exhausted. It wasn't just the journey to London and back, nor the socialising, nor her conversation with Nina. She didn't blame Nina for what had happened. She blamed herself. She had allowed her emotions to take over and she had compromised her principles. Well, never again. Jake had conned her. He had promised her what she wanted to hear and then done the opposite.

Why? Why? her heart cried. A more practical consideration was what she was going to do now. She could no longer work on the project. She could not bear to see Jake. Polly closed her eyes, feeling the comforting vibration of the bus engine reverberating on the glass against her cheek as she slid gently into sleep. Tomorrow she would phone Neil and tell him she was ill. She would not be going back to Green Lives until Jacob Grayling had returned to London forever.

The bus arrived at Glasgow Buchanan Street station at seven o'clock in the morning. Tired, grey-faced passengers descended and stood huddled and yawning before catching taxis or meeting friends and family. Soon only Polly was left in the terminal. She hesitated. She could return home to her flat in the City. But Keisha's cousins would be there. She had invited them over when she learned that Polly would be in London. Polly could not face the thought of company. She wanted somewhere quiet to lick her wounds and heal her heart so that she could face the world with confidence again.

She sat in the bus terminal building nursing a coffee which grew cold over a couple of hours. She did not seem to have the energy to move. Her mobile phone rang.

'Polly, where are you? Harriet phoned me to say you left London last night.' Lou's voice sounded at once concerned and yet curiously bright.

'Yes, I . . . '

'Look, never mind now, come and tell me all about it in person. I'm at Mum and Dad's. We're having a bit of a celebration.'

'What are you celebrating?' Polly was relieved to hear Lou sound so normal, so happy, but what could have happened while she was away?

'Come on, if you're at your flat you can be here in less than an hour. We'll have coffee and cakes waiting!'

Lou rang off. Polly frowned at her phone. What was going on? Then she shouldered her weekend bag and an anticipation of comfort, home cooking and tender loving care from her mum made her sigh with relief, and head for the subway and her flat. The car was parked there. She wouldn't even need to go inside to see Keisha. The car keys were in her handbag. Yes, she would be in company — but it would be her family and that was an entirely different thing.

The journey north was smooth and pleasant with minimal traffic, the fields dotted with little puffs of white lambs, the melodious call of willow warblers floating through the open window as she approached her parents' house on a road that broke through willow thickets. The crunch of gravel as she parked had Laura flinging the door of the house open and running to her, arms outstretched.

'What a welcome. And how's my favourite niece?' Polly swung the little girl up high, enjoying her happy shrieks.

'Daddy's home and he brought me a 'normous teddy!'

Lou appeared on the doorstep, grinning. She winked at Polly as Ian arrived to stand beside her with his arm around her possessively. So that was what the celebrations were about. The prodigal husband.

'Long time, no see,' said Polly coolly. She wasn't letting him off that easily. He had made Lou miserable and he had to pay.

Ian had the grace to look embarrassed and shuffled his feet, coughing.

'Don't be mean, now, please, Polly,' warned Lou, giving her husband a warm embrace before they turned back together into the hallway.

Polly shook her head in bafflement. Lou seemed to have completely forgotten how much she had cried when Ian was away, and her fear that he would never come back. Her ability to defend his actions even when he was clearly (in Polly's eyes) in the wrong was surprising.

It is called love, a voice said inside her head. *And if you love Jake, why do you doubt him? You never even gave him a chance to explain.*

How could he explain his complete turnaround on the designs? Anyway, he was engaged to Nina by now. She was welcome to him. Polly shut the voice out and refused to listen. She would add him to her list of disastrous love affairs and carry on. She didn't need a man. She had a career and a loving family and that was enough.

'You look pale,' her mum said as she

hugged her. 'Go on in to the living room and chat to your dad while I bring you some coffee. You must have some cake to build you up. There's cherry sponge or lemon drizzle. Which do you want? Or a slice of both?'

Polly could still hear her describing the food as she entered the living room and found her father. He was sitting reading the newspaper, which he put down carefully to look at her.

'It's a mistake, looking so wan,' he said. 'Now your mother won't let you leave before you are at least a stone heavier.'

Polly laughed and hugged him hard. It was good to be home.

When they were all seated with steaming cups of aromatic coffee, Polly asked wickedly, 'So, what's the celebration?'

Lou cut in quickly before their parents had time to query Polly's question.

'Spring, life, family. It's good to be alive.'

'It is indeed,' said Ian, in a heartfelt

tone, clasping Lou's hand.

Mrs Baker smiled at them fondly. Polly was pierced by a sudden, unwelcome shaft of envy. Lou and Ian had it all. It was as if an invisible bubble surrounded them, filled with love. Add Laura to that bubble and they needed nothing more. Yes, they had their ups and downs, their problems like any other couple, but their strong devotion to one another helped them survive and overcome them all.

'How was the London trip?' Mrs Baker asked, settling herself more comfortably into the sofa and offering the plate of cake around again.

'It was okay.'

'Just okay? What about the ball? I want to hear what the ladies were wearing and what you had to eat.'

'Can we do it later, Mum?' said Polly. 'I'm tired.'

There was an awkward silence. Mrs Baker brushed a crumb off her lap. Mr Baker leant over and patted Polly's knee.

'Relax, eat some of your mother's delicious baking and have a snooze if you wish in front of the fire. It works for me every time.'

They all laughed in relief, and the moment passed. Ian and Lou decided to take Laura for a walk and went off to find wellies and coats. Mrs Baker disappeared to the kitchen to wrap some snacks for them. Polly and her dad sat companionably, watching the flickering flames and listening to the comforting sound of crackling wood and spitting coal.

The doorbell rang. Polly heard it vaguely through her reverie. She didn't budge, thinking it would be Mel and Isla, who often appeared for coffee and to pass on the latest gossip.

The living room door opened and she half turned to greet 'the girls'. Her smile died. Jake stood there, dishevelled, face lean and unshaven, blue eyes wary and tired. Polly got to her feet weakly.

'Isn't this a nice surprise?' Mrs Baker

said, ushering Jake further into the room. Polly felt the familiar prickle of electricity at his closeness. She could have reached out and stroked his hair.

'Cup of coffee?' her mother went on. Polly could see she was about to launch into Jake's baking options. She opened her mouth to say something, anything, to get him to go, when Jake spoke.

'I hope you'll forgive me, Mrs Baker, if I don't stay. I just came to take Polly for a walk.'

The last thing Polly wanted was a walk with Jacob Grayling but he had a strong grip and was already guiding her gently but firmly towards the hall and the bright day outside.

Neither spoke until they were on the trail through the fields. Polly wondered whether they were heading for Ben Dhubh or for Claxton Farm. What did it matter? Her heart was doing its strange dance again. Jake's proximity had that effect on her while her head insisted that it was useless and a waste of time to feel that way.

Suddenly he spun round on her. Polly took a step back, shocked at the spark of anger in his eyes.

'Why did you go?' he demanded, sounding annoyed and bewildered in equal parts. 'I waited and waited in the Gold Room. You never showed up and then Harriet ran in saying you'd gone home. I got the first flight possible to find you.'

Polly felt her own temper rise. How dare he follow her here to challenge her, when he was the one in the wrong!

'I trusted you,' she cried. 'The eco-village. Remember? Or were you too caught up in your profit margin to think of the designs we agreed upon?'

He winced at the scorn in her voice, then rubbed his face as if puzzled.

'That's what I wanted to show you in the Gold Room.'

'I saw them myself. Nina took me there and showed me how you had crammed in all that extra housing. You've destroyed it all, Jake. I hope it makes you really proud.'

'Nina? What has she to do with it?'

'Nina. Your fiancée. Congratulations. You make a perfect couple,' Polly said bitingly. She flung herself away from him and stumbled down the trail, tears falling hotly on her cheeks.

'My fiancée? Polly, wait!'

Polly started to run, the grassy trail blurring. Jake caught her easily, pulling her to him. She felt the strength of him, the warmth of his tall body, the desire to melt into him. His body was shuddering. For a moment she thought he was crying, then his laughter rang out into the summer air, startling a couple of rooks into the sky from the nearby tussocks.

'You are an idiot, Polly Baker,' he said, not letting her go. Polly stopped struggling and stared up at him. She waited.

'The extra buildings you saw on the designs, the blocks overshadowing the Loch, are eco-buildings on stilts. The loch will be intact while each house and the Visitor Centre will be run for energy efficiency and be as green as possible.'

'Visitor Centre?'

'I thought you'd be delighted with that extra touch. People can come to find out about the wildlife on the loch and about the eco-village. It will be the first of its kind and will set a positive agenda for future housing to combat global warming.'

'Now you sound like a brochure.'

'That's the first paragraph of the brochure,' Jake grinned. He handed her his neatly folded handkerchief.

Polly blew her nose loudly.

'As for Nina,' Jake continued, 'I'm sure she would love to be my fiancée but I have no desire for a wife who only wants me for my wealth and status. I want a wife who loves me and is happy to live in a small Scottish farmhouse out of the glare of publicity.'

'Jake,' Polly said, then paused. Her head was spinning. Jake was not in love with Nina. He was not engaged to be married to her. Best of all, he had not betrayed her trust.

'I'm so sorry that I didn't trust you,' she said slowly. 'I saw the sketches, listened to Nina, and made two and two add up to five.'

'From the first moment I saw you, submerged in the middle of Monmeir Loch, I knew you were trouble,' Jake told her. 'You just need me here to take care of you.'

He bent to kiss her and Polly knew that she need not compromise on love after all. She loved Jake with all of her heart; forever.

★ ★ ★

Amy Baker Grayling was playing with her cousin Katy. The game involved flinging daisies at each other, which was fine until one hit Amy in the eye. She howled. Polly picked her up and comforted her.

'Want Daddy,' Amy cried.

Polly kissed the top of her daughter's head soothingly and looked across the field to where the barbecue was set up

186

near the farmhouse. Jake and Ian were hunched over the smoking grill, poking at bits of scorched meat and unidentifiable black lumps. Mrs Baker and Shanna Grayling were doing their best to pretend not to notice, and were smiling over the tops of their champagne glasses at each other and chatting while reclining comfortably on the easy chairs. Mr Baker was visible in the distance, binoculars pointed to the sky where some dark speck of a bird circled hopefully.

Lou scooped up Katy, who was sniffling now too.

'Do they need help? It would be nice if there were some sausages ready for the children to eat.'

'Perhaps we should rescue them. Here comes Laura to play, Amy.'

Laura ran across the grass towards them. Amy, her mood switched completely from despair to joy at the sight of her cousin, wriggled to be free and set off on chubby legs to meet her. Katy ran with her.

Polly and Lou linked arms and walked over to the barbecue.

Shanna Grayling raised her glass at their approach. 'Well, here's to Croombs Wood.'

The sisters grabbed their glasses, hastily filled by Jake. Mr Baker had returned from his birdwatching. Ian had subdued the barbecued meat and found his own champagne glass filled. Then the family raised their glasses in a heartfelt toast to the woods.

'I can't believe it's taken three years to get the road halted,' said Jake, shaking his head.

'It's thanks to your effort that it went to a public enquiry,' said Polly to her husband proudly.

Jake had been profoundly moved by his experience that day at Croombs Wood, watching people experience nature in their local green space. It had changed his perspective on development forever, and opened his mind to new concepts of open space dynamics where building and architecture were involved. Above all, that day he realised how deeply he loved Polly and the memory of their picnic was precious indeed.

'How is the Monmeir Eco-Village going?' asked Mr Baker, 'I saw a long article in the Herald about it. They were singing its praises. Talking about further villages to come. Nice picture of Jake with the village and loch in the background.'

Jake opened his mouth to speak. Ian, Lou and Polly all groaned.

'Dad, don't start him on his favourite subject,' begged Polly. 'He's completely forgotten that I had to persuade him to build it, and now considers it his project right from the start!'

'He should be proud,' said her father seriously. 'The wildlife is flourishing and according to the papers, the village is carbon neutral. I must visit myself, see what the birdlife is like.'

Jake winked at Polly. She glared at him, mock angrily. He refilled her champagne glass to the brim and she grinned. Mr Baker, watching them, shook his head and smiled. He cleaned the lenses of his binoculars.

Birds were so simple, unlike human beings. They flew, they ate, they displayed, they sang and bred. They were easy to read, unlike his family. Once the barbecue was finished he would walk across the fields to his own house and make a count of the birds as they came in to roost. Then he and Polly and Lou's mother could sit companionably over a cup of tea and discuss the day's events as was their wont.

'Where is my beautiful granddaughter?' asked Shanna.

Polly looked back at the field anxiously. Motherhood, though wonderful, was fraught with fear. When she confessed this, her own mother had cheerfully told her she would never be free from it. It came with the territory.

'Mummy, Daddy, I got a beastie,' piped a little voice excitedly. Amy, Katy and Laura appeared from the side of

Claxton Farm, Amy's hands scooped carefully round some small treasure.

'Definitely your daughter,' said Jake. He kissed his wife tenderly on her brow.

'I'm going to make it a little house to live in,' added Amy.

'And yours,' said Polly wickedly, kissing Jake back.

THE END

We do hope that you have enjoyed reading this large print book.

Did you know that all of our titles are available for purchase?

We publish a wide range of high quality large print books including:
Romances, Mysteries, Classics
General Fiction
Non Fiction and Westerns

Special interest titles available in large print are:
The Little Oxford Dictionary
Music Book, Song Book
Hymn Book, Service Book

Also available from us courtesy of Oxford University Press:
Young Readers' Dictionary
(large print edition)
Young Readers' Thesaurus
(large print edition)

For further information or a free brochure, please contact us at:
Ulverscroft Large Print Books Ltd.,
The Green, Bradgate Road, Anstey,
Leicester, LE7 7FU, England.
Tel: (00 44) **0116 236 4325**
Fax: (00 44) **0116 234 0205**

TOMORROW'S DREAMS

Chrissie Loveday

Nellie is a talented paintress in the pottery industry of the 1920s. Disaster strikes the family, and she becomes the main breadwinner for her parents and three siblings. But the fates conspire against her and she is forced to seek employment where she can find it. She loses her heart to the wrong man and he, recognising her special talents, offers her a future. But how could she ever move into his world?

TO LOVE AGAIN

Fenella Miller

Since she was widowed, it has been difficult for Emma Reed and her young children, Jack and Mary. But then, Rupert Bucknall offers her a job as his housekeeper. However things do not go well. Rupert has a fearsome temper and doesn't want her or the children to remain. Since his accident Rupert has lived as a recluse, believing his scars make him hideous. But Emma, with nowhere to go, must persuade Mr Bucknall that she is indispensable.